D1590625

THE GUNSMITH

470

Gunsmith for Sale

Books by J.R. Roberts
(Robert J. Randisi)

The Gunsmith series

Gunsmith Giant series

Lady Gunsmith series

Angel Eyes series

Tracker series

Mountain Jack Pike series

COMING SOON!
The Gunsmith
471 – A Price on a Gunsmith's Head

For more information visit:
www.SpeakingVolumes.us

THE GUNSMITH

470

Gunsmith for Sale

J. R. Roberts

WITHDRAWN FROM
RA̶   ̶̶̶RARY

PARISH LIBRARY
Alexandria, Louisiana JN

SPEAKING VOLUMES, LLC
NAPLES, FLORIDA
2021

Gunsmith for Sale

Copyright © 2021 by Robert J. Randisi

All rights reserved. No part of this book may be reproduced or transmitted in any form or by any means.

ISBN 978-1-64540-489-7

Chapter One

Clint Adams stared across the desk at the manager of the First Bank of Westfield, Kansas.

"Say that again," he said.

"Mr. Adams, we contacted your bank, and they inform us that—well, your account is empty."

"That can't be," Clint said.

"I'm sorry," Walter Davis, the manager, said. "It states that quite plainly, here." He handed Clint the telegram. Clint read it and handed it back.

"I don't care what it says there," he replied. "It can't be right."

"I'm sorry," Davis repeated, "there's nothing I can do."

Clint stood up.

"I'll just send some telegrams of my own," he said. "I'll get this straightened out."

"I hope so—" Davis started, but Clint turned and stormed out.

***

Clint had arrived in Westfield, Kansas a couple of days earlier. At the time he had enough money in his pockets for what he wanted to do, which wasn't much.

He wanted a room, a stall for his horse, a drink and a meal. He got all of those the first day, then walked around town the following morning and found that he liked the place. It was a fairly large town, still growing, with plenty of businesses—including hotels and saloons—a newspaper, bank and telegraph office. It had a couple of interesting looking restaurants he planned to try.

He spent several days eating, drinking, even playing some poker. And he met Lily Claire.

Lily had been eating alone in one of the restaurants, a place called The Porterhouse. Since Clint was also alone, and the two had noticed each other, he decided to be straightforward. While both of them waited to be served their food, he rose and walked to her table.

"I hope you don't mind," he said, "but you look like a lady who doesn't like to eat alone."

She did look like a lady. She was wearing a purple dress with earrings that matched, and her make-up was expertly applied to a lovely face. From across the room he had thought her to be in her late twenties, but up close he saw she was in her mid-thirties. That actually suited him more.

"Quite the contrary," she said to him. "I actually like eating alone."

"Oh, I see," he said. "Excuse me—"

"But tonight," she went on, "I can make an exception. Please, sit."

"Thank you."

Clint waved at the waiter and asked him to please bring his meal at the same time as the lady's.

They ate together and learned a little about each other. She was a widow who lived in a house in an expensive part of town. When he introduced himself, she immediately recognized his name, and smiled, saying now she was very glad to have made that exception. If she was going to have company over dinner, she preferred it to be someone interesting.

After the meal Clint insisted on paying, so she insisted he come to her house for a drink. The nightcap turned into the entire evening.

She gave him a glass of sherry, they drank, and then kissed. The kiss went on for a long time until he reached behind her back. The dress came off easily. The undergarments took a little longer until, laughing, she helped him remove everything until she was naked.

She was full-bodied and solid, the way he liked his women now that he was also getting older. Younger, slimmer women didn't have much appeal for him, anymore.

She led him to her bedroom where he removed his gunbelt, set it within easy reach, and then took care of the rest of his clothes while she watched from the bed. She lounged on her side with her head cocked, enjoying the show.

When he joined her, she wrapped her arms and legs around him and said in a husky voice, "I was thinking about this moment when I first saw you enter the restaurant."

"I'm glad we're here, then," he said.

He kissed her again, then freed himself from her grasp so he could roam her body with his hands and mouth.

"Mmm," she moaned, as he worked his way down and nestled between her thighs, "I had the feeling you'd know how to handle a woman."

"You know," he said, "you seem to have a knack for telling the future." He touched the moist lips of her vagina, which caused her to start, as if his touch was electric. "Tell me what you think is going to happen next."

Without waiting for an answer, he began to work on her with his mouth and tongue.

Chapter Two

That was their first night together. He bought dinner the second night, this time at an even more expensive restaurant called The Harvest. He also ran into some bad luck, which only confirmed his previous intention not to play poker anymore—at least, not for a while.

But because of the poker losses, the expensive meals, drinks at the Northern Saloon, he had gone to the bank to withdraw some money on his third day in town. He knew the teller would have to contact his Denver bank, so he gave the young man the information, and said he'd return later in the day. When he came back, the teller told him the manager wanted to see him, and that was when he learned that his account was supposedly empty.

He left the bank, fuming, and went directly to the telegraph office. After sending off several telegrams, he walked to the Northern Saloon. Luckily, he still had enough money in his pocket for a beer.

"You look like somebody killed yer dog," the bartender said, when he set the beer down.

"Something like that."

"Wanna talk about it?"

"No, thanks."

The bartender shrugged and walked away.

Clint turned his back to the bar, leaned against it, beer in hand, and looked around. It was getting on toward dusk. Businesses were closing for the day, and people were coming in to drink, or play, or both. A couple of men at the poker table nodded to him, and he nodded back but made no attempt to join them. For a change, he had found some townspeople who were actually good poker players.

He had a second beer, stayed in the saloon for about an hour, then left and headed to his hotel. He had instructed the telegraph operator to deliver any replies there.

He went directly to the front desk.

"Can I help you, Mr. Adams?" the middle-aged desk clerk asked.

"I'm waiting for some telegrams," Clint said.

"Ah, yes." The man turned and put his hand in the slot for Clint's room. He came out with two yellow slips.

"There you are."

The first was from his partners in the saloon his friend Rick had started in Mission City, Texas before his death. The telegrams assured him that his share of the profits was being deposited into his bank account every week. He had no reason to believe it was a lie.

The second was from the First National Bank of Denver. It informed him that the money in his account had all been withdrawn, as per his instructions. But he had sent no such instructions. Now he had something else to investigate. But he'd have to wait til morning to send another telegram.

He went to his room, sat on the bed and counted his money. He had enough for two more nights in the hotel, three if he didn't eat or drink anything, again. This was a very odd situation for him. It had been a long time since money was any kind of problem. He had several businesses around the country that brought money into his accounts.

The immediate problem was that he was supposed to have another meal with Lily that night. And, of course she would probably expect him to pick up the bill. He couldn't very well tell her that he was too broke to do that.

He grabbed his saddlebag, reached inside, rummaged around, and came out with an emergency stash of bills. There was less there than he had thought, but certainly enough to pay for one more supper. If he was forced to remain in Westfield, Kansas any longer, he was going to have to find a source of income. The only way he was going to get to Denver was to pay his way.

He washed, changed his clothes, and went out to meet Lily for supper.

***

Lily Claire opened her front door to leave the house and go meet Clint Adams but stopped short when she saw the man standing there.

"You look like you're in a hurry," the tall, handsome man said.

"I am, Freddy," she said. "Sorry."

She tried to get by him, but he grabbed hold of her elbow.

"Seems like you're always too busy for me these days, Lily," he observed.

"I'm too busy for you any day, Freddy," she said. "I've told you that."

He tightened his grip.

"You can't keep treating me like this," he hissed.

"You're hurting my arm!"

Abruptly, he released her, as if the touch of her had burned him.

"We have to talk, Lily," he insisted.

"We have nothing to talk about, Freddy," she said. "Now excuse me, I have to go."

She locked her front door and headed down the walk to the street. He gave her a head start, then followed.

Chapter Three

Clint hesitated before entering The Harvest, the most expensive eatery in town. Lily's expensive tastes had not been a problem the first couple of times they ate together. It was amazing how quickly things could change.

He decided to bite the bullet—and perhaps chicken rather than steak—and went inside. Lily was already seated at the same table they'd had last time.

He gave her a gentlemanly peck on the cheek and sat across from her. When the waiter came Clint was about to order a chicken dinner, which was the cheapest thing on the menu, when Lily spoke up.

"I think it's time I bought you a meal," she said, "don't you?"

"If you insist," he said. "And if it's not an ungentle-manly thing for me to let you do."

She leaned forward and said, "You've been ungen-tlemanly enough in the bedroom."

"You think so?" he asked. "Wait until later."

"Lord a-mighty," she said, in a contrived Southern accent, while fanning herself, "I declare!"

The waiter tried to ignore their sexual fencing and took down their orders for steak dinners.

"What's that?" Clint asked, pointing to her bare left arm.

"What?" she asked, looking down.

"You have bruises on your arm," he said, pointing. "In fact, they look like finger marks."

"Oh, that." She closed her right hand over her left arm to hide them. "It's nothing."

"Who did that to you?"

"Just a man in town who thinks he's entitled to something he's not."

"Do you need help with him?" he asked.

Inadvertently, she looked over at the window.

"What? Is he outside?" Clint asked. "Did he follow you here?"

"I—I don't think so."

"Who is it, Lily?"

"I—I don't think I should tell you."

"Why not?"

"I don't want you to do anything that would get you into trouble."

"Me?" he asked, innocently. "What would I do to get myself in trouble?"

"Shoot him," she said.

"Would you mind if I shot him?"

11

"Like I said," she replied, "I don't want you to get into trouble, but no, I wouldn't mind, at all."

"Then tell me his name and where I can find him."

"Let's eat," she said, "and talk about this later."

"All right."

Clint wouldn't have minded being able to take out his frustration on somebody. This man who had bruised Lily's arm seemed a good choice.

***

Frederick Collins had, indeed, followed Lily to the Harvest Restaurant. He watched through the window as she was joined by a man who kissed her cheek. Collins felt his face suffuse with blood. Who did this man think he was?

As the two sat across from each other and talked, Freddy Collins wondered how he could go about finding out who this man was? He decided to just wait there for them to come out and follow him. He had a small der-ringer in his pocket, so maybe he'd even kill the man. That would teach Lily a lesson she wouldn't forget.

***

Clint and Lily enjoyed their steaks—especially Clint who, for the moment, didn't have to worry about his lack of funds. He did feel bad, allowing Lily to pay tonight's bill, but there wasn't much he could do about it at the moment.

"Dessert?" she asked him, when they had finished.

"No," he said, thinking it was the least he could do, turning down dessert. "I'll wait until we get to your place for that."

"Clint Adams!" she chided. "You're a bad man."

"This bad man thinks we ought to get going," he said.

Lily paid the bill, and she and Clint left the Harvest and walked to her buggy. Clint's Tobiano pony, Toby, was still in the livery stable.

Clint helped her up into the seat, then climbed in next to her and picked up the reins.

"Mind if I hitch a ride?" he asked.

She put her hand on his arm and said, "I don't mind, at all."

As they drove off, Freddy Collins did his best to follow them on foot.

Chapter Four

When they got to her house, Lily poured two glasses of sherry before they went into her bedroom. They sat together in the living room to have their drinks.

"Are you going to get around to telling me who bruised your arm?" Clint asked.

Lily heaved a sigh, then began talking.

"His name is Frederick Collins. He's a businessman in town, used to work with my husband. When Edward died, Freddy thought he would step right in and take up where my husband left off."

"And you told him no?"

"I certainly did," she said, "and I've been telling him no for three years now."

"But he won't accept it?"

"He thinks he's an important man, and I should acknowledge that," she said. "What he doesn't know is that the touch of his hand makes my skin crawl."

"Then you should tell him that," Clint said.

"I don't want to be cruel," she said, "but I think you're probably right."

"Sometimes being cruel is the only way to get your point across," he told her.

"Well," she said, putting her glass down, "I'm not feeling very cruel tonight."

She moved closer to him on the sofa . . .

***

Freddy Collins was lurking outside. He was out of breath and sweaty from trying to keep up with Lily's buggy. Luckily, they hadn't driven it very fast. But this wasn't what an important businessman like Freddy was supposed to be doing. He felt foolish, sneaking around in the dark outside Lily's house. What was wrong with this woman? Didn't she know they belonged together?

Collins decided to go home. Tomorrow he would come up with an entirely fresh plan on how to handle Lily Claire.

***

Clint broke the kiss and turned his head to look at the window.

"What is it?" Lily asked.

"Somebody was outside the house," he said, "but he's gone now."

"How do you know?"

"I can feel it," Clint said, looking at her. "And didn't you see him following us back here?"

"Who? Freddy?"

"There was no way I could know who he was," Clint said. "I just knew someone was following on foot, that's why I drove so slow."

"Why didn't you just drive faster and lose him?" she asked. "It would have been easy."

"I wanted to see what he would do," Clint said, "find out what kind of man he is."

"And what did you find out?"

"He skulks around in the dark," Clint said, "probably trying to peek in a window. But whether he saw anything or not, he left."

"Freddy would never face you," she said, "even if he doesn't know who you are."

"Well," Clint said, "we don't have to give him any more thought tonight."

"No," she said, "tonight is just for us."

She rose from the sofa, took his hands and tugged him to his feet. Then she kissed him and led him to the bedroom.

***

Later, Clint got out of bed without waking her, took his clothes to the living room and got dressed. His glass of sherry was still on the table in front of the sofa. He sat down and drank it. He put the empty glass on the table next to hers and left the house. He stopped just outside, on the porch, and looked around—not only with his eyes, but with all his senses. He didn't see, feel or smell anything out of the ordinary.

He could have taken her buggy back to the hotel, but it wasn't out front where they had left it. Apparently, she had somebody put the buggy and horse away for her.

Westfield was too large to get from one end to the other. He walked a few blocks to a larger street, where he was able to find a horse drawn cab to take him back to his hotel.

When he walked into the lobby the desk clerk waved at him with a telegram in his hand.

"Another one," he said, handing it over.

"Thanks."

Clint waited until he was in his room before opening the telegram.

It was from Denver.

Chapter Five

He had tried to get hold of his friend, Talbot Roper, in Denver, but the telegram informed him that Roper was out of town on a case. That meant he was going to have to go to Denver himself to check with his bank. All he had to do was amass the funds to get there. Train fare for himself and his horse was not cheap.

He set the telegram aside and turned in.

***

The next morning he had a cheap breakfast in the hotel dining room, while he thought over his situation.

He could borrow some money from Lily, who had been left quite well-off when her husband died. But asking her would just be too embarrassing.

So where did that leave him? He was going to have to take some kind of job that would pay him enough to get him to Denver. And the talent that he had to trade on was his ability with guns, both shooting them plus repairing and/or building them.

He didn't have time to build somebody a gun, so he needed to find somebody who needed a gun repaired.

He still wasn't willing to hire himself out as a bounty hunter or gunman.

It was too bad he had started a dalliance with Lily Claire. If she had simply hired him to help her fend off her unwanted suitor, his problem would be solved.

He also knew it was possible that he was going to have to take some odd jobs to work his way to Denver. It remained to be seen if he could find one that would fund the entire trip.

He couldn't ask his partners in Mission City to send him money. They had already deposited his share in the bank, and it wasn't their fault that the money had somehow disappeared. He could've sent telegrams to Bat Masterson or Luke Short to send him some money. But he didn't know where they were, at the moment.

By the end of breakfast, he knew that he was on his own with this problem. After all, he was the guy everybody else came to for help, not the guy who went to others. And he didn't want anyone to know about his situation.

He decided to go out and buy a copy of the most recent issue of Westfield's newspaper, *The Courier*. Sometimes people put notices in a newspaper when they needed to hire some help.

***

He had to go directly to the newspaper office for a copy of the latest edition. As he entered, a grey-haired fellow working on the printing press looked up at him. He was frowning and had black smudges on his face.

"Trouble?" Clint asked.

"Always," the man said. "Damn thing never works right." He stepped away from the press and grabbed a nearby towel. "I'm Mitchell, the editor and press operator. What can I do for you? Advertising?"

"No," Clint said, "I'd just like to see your recent edition. Couldn't find one around town, anywhere."

"We run weekly," the man said. "We're supposed to come out tomorrow."

"Do you have any from last week?"

"Of course we do," Mitchell said. "Lord knows I always print too many."

"Good," Clint said.

"Why do you want it?"

"I'm lookin' for a job," Clint explained. "Thought I might find something in the paper."

"Well, you might, at that," Mitchell said. "I'll get you a copy."

"I'd appreciate it."

The man went into a back room, taking the towel with him, and returned with a copy of the newspaper.

"Here you go," he said, handing it to Clint.

"Much obliged."

"What kind of thing are you looking for?" the man asked. "Something permanent?"

"No," Clint said, "something quick."

"Tell me," Mitchell said, "you don't happen to operate a printing press, do you?"

"Sorry, no."

"Ah, too bad. Well, I hope you find something in there."

"Thanks for your help," Clint said, and left the office.

Chapter Six

Clint took the newspaper to his hotel, sat in a chair out front and leafed through it. He didn't bother reading any of the news stories. He was only looking for some sort of ad or listing for a job. There wasn't much, but he did find something that interested him. Apparently, the local gunsmith advertised his services in the paper. He noticed the location, left the paper on the chair and started walking.

***

The sign over the door simply said GUNSMITH SHOP. On the window it said: ALL GUNSMITHING SERVICES AVAILABLE.

He went inside and was immediately comforted by the smells of gun oil, iron and gunpowder. There was a grizzled old man behind the counter, working on a gun, with a set of telescopic glasses perched on his head like a visor. He was squinting through the lenses while he worked and abruptly looked up as Clint entered.

"What can I do fer you, friend?" he asked, removing the glasses and setting them down on the counter.

"I saw your advertisement in the paper," Clint said. "I wondered if you had any work."

"You a gunsmith?" the man asked.

"I am."

"Any good?"

"I haven't done it in a while, but I was good, yeah," Clint said.

"Well," the man said, "I ain't really got enough work for myself, which is why I took the ad. Sorry, fella."

"What's your name, sir?" Clint asked.

"My name's Jared Whitaker," the man said. "Ain't nobody called me 'sir' in a long time."

"Well, Jared, my name's Clint Adams, and—"

"Well, hell's bells, man!" Jared said. "You ain't *a* gunsmith, you're *the* Gunsmith! What the hell are you doin' in town?"

"Passing through, really, but I've sort of had a run of bad luck. I thought I might just pick up a few dollars doing some work for you."

"Well," Jared said, "like I said, I ain't got enough work for me, but maybe we could do some kind of deal."

"What did you have in mind?" Clint asked, with interest.

"Well," Jared said, rubbing his jaw, "that gun on your hip, for one thing."

Clint looked down at the Peacemaker he'd been wearing for years. Long before the Colt company had come up with the double-action revolver, he had modified his own gun. The weapon had been ahead of its time.

"I'll buy it from ya," Jared said.

"My gun?" Clint said.

"Unless you got somethin' else to sell me," Jared said. "Your horse? Saddle?"

"No," Clint said, "I couldn't do that." He thought about the Colt New Line he kept in his saddlebag as a backup. But if he could get a decent amount of money for his Peacemaker, it might just finance the entire trip to Denver.

"I wouldn't wanna leave you without a gun, ya know," Jared said. "I could throw in a trade." He looked at Clint's hip. "I ain't interested in the holster, just the gun."

He figured if he gave up the gun, he still had the New Line and his rifle. After he straightened his finances out, he could buy himself a new gun, or even make himself one. On the other hand, this Peacemaker had been with him for years, and fit his hand just right.

"Well," he said to the old man, "let's see what you've got . . ."

***

After trying to pawn off some older weapons on Clint, the gunsmith came up with a newer model .45 Schofield, from Smith & Wesson. It was similar to Colt's .45 but fired a shorter cartridge with a larger rim. It was manufactured at the suggestion of Major George Schofield and so named for him. The lighter cartridge was made for a gun that was fired more accurately by the troops. Patented in 1871, by 1879 the U.S. Army had purchased over 8200 of them.

"I got this in just a few weeks ago," Jared said, setting the pistol down on the counter. "Since then I broke it down, cleaned it and put it back together. It's the eighteen-seventy-seven model."

"Accurate?"

"To within a hair."

"I'll have to try it," Clint said.

"It's loaded."

Clint picked it up, hefted its weight approvingly.

"Do you have a target?"

"In the back room."

Together they walked to the back, and Clint saw a bullseye at the far end of the room attached to a bale of hay.

"The hay will prevent any unfortunate ricochets," Jared explained.

Clint only had to fire the gun at the target twice, hitting the bullseye both times.

"Fine shootin'," Jared said.

"You're right," Clint said. "It shoots just a hair to the left."

"I'm sure you can fix that," Jared said.

Clint turned and looked at the older man, then said, "All right, let's talk money."

***

Clint left the gunsmith shop with money in his pocket, and the Schofield in his holster. The gun felt lighter on his hip and would take some getting used to.

The gunsmith, Jared Whittaker, was also quite pleased with his purchase/trade. Clint was sure he planned to display the gun, possibly in his window, letting everyone know that it was the Gunsmith's gun.

With the money he now had, he could leave Westfield, ride to Kansas City and catch a train. He wouldn't need to take as many odd jobs as he'd been afraid he would. Might even arrive in Denver sooner than he figured and get all this bank business figured out.

Chapter Seven

"You're leaving when?" Lily asked, at supper.

"Tomorrow morning."

"So soon?"

"Something's come up," he said, "and I have to go and look into it."

"It can't wait a few more days?" she asked.

"I wish it could," he said. "Why, is there something in particular you need me for?"

"Beyond the obvious?" she said. "Yes. I had another incident with Freddy this morning, as I was leaving the house. He was demanding to know who you are."

"Did you tell him?"

"I certainly did," she said. "I told him it was none of his business." She rubbed her hands. "He tried to get handsy, again."

"I suppose I could have a talk with him before I leave," he said.

"I wish you would," she said. "Once you do leave, I'm afraid he'll take that as a sign."

"Well," Clint said, "let's see if I can give him an altogether different sign. Just tell me where to find him."

***

Lily told Clint where Frederick Collins' office was. Located on the corner of two busy streets, in crossing, he had to dodge a couple of wagons, some horses, and a few citizens to get to the other side of the street. Yes, Westfield was a busy town.

The building that housed Frederick Collins Inc. was two stories high, and Lily told him the office was on the second floor. He went up, found the door that said F. Collins Inc., and entered. A woman seated at a desk looked up from whatever she was doing and frowned. She had grey hair and wire-framed glasses.

"Can I help you?"

"I'd like to see Mr. Collins."

"And what's it about?"

"It's a private matter."

"Well," she said, "this is a business office."

"Then you ask him if he wants his personal business mixed in with his professional business," Clint suggested.

She heaved a sigh.

"Very well. Wait here." She stood and went to the other door in the room. She knocked and entered, then returned momentarily.

"You can go in," she said, returning to her desk. She had left the door ajar.

"Thank you," he said.

When he entered, the man behind the desk looked at him, and Clint saw recognition on his face. He stood immediately, revealing himself to be six-feet tall. He was probably in his forties, but his face had so many lines it was hard to tell. This, Clint thought, was not a man Lily or any other woman would want to be with, at first glance.

"What do you want?" he demanded.

"Do you know who I am?" Clint asked.

"I only know you've been sniffing around Lily," Collins said. "I don't like it."

"My name is Clint Adams."

The man hesitated, then said, "Clint . . . wait, Adams?"

"Now do you know who I am?"

The man swallowed and nodded.

"Then sit down and shut up," Clint ordered.

The man meekly did what he was told.

"You put bruises on Lily's arm," Clint said. "If you ever do that again, I'll put bruises all over you. Understand?"

Collins nodded.

"And you've been bothering her," Clint said. "That has to stop. Don't go to her house anymore, and don't approach her on the street, or a café . . . anywhere. Do you understand?"

"Um, yes," Collins said.

"I don't ever want to see you again," Clint said, "so don't give me any reasons to come calling. Got it?"

"I've got it," Collins said, quietly.

Clint turned, headed for the door, then turned back.

"And get yourself a new receptionist," he said, "this one's rude."

Collins just nodded.

Clint left the man's office, ignored the cold look of the receptionist, hoping he had managed to get her fired.

***

After Clint Adams left his office, Freddy Collins took a deep breath, then grabbed a bottle of whiskey from his desk drawer and drank directly from the bottle. How the hell had Lily gotten herself involved with the Gunsmith? And why didn't she tell him? He could have said the wrong thing to the man and gotten himself killed. And Lily Claire was not worth getting killed over.

He had another drink.

Chapter Eight

Lily said she appreciated what Clint had done. After one more night together, she decided not to see him off in the morning.

"I hate goodbyes," she said. "Any chance you'll ever come back?"

Clint thought about his gun over at Jared Whitaker's and said, "It's not impossible."

He rode out in the morning, heading for Kansas City.

***

Upon arrival in Kansas City he stopped at the railroad station to purchase passage for himself and his Tobiano.

"Tomorrow morning," the clerk told him.

"Nothing sooner?"

"Sorry."

That meant a hotel for him and a livery stall for Toby. And then a meal. Luckily, he still had plenty of the money from the sale of his gun.

***

On the train, during the ride, he found himself reaching down and touching the Schofield in his holster, missing his Peacemaker. But he had to stop touching the gun, because it was making some of the passengers—most notably the ones sitting across from him—nervous.

When the train arrived in Kansas City's Union Station he disembarked and claimed Toby from the stock car. He had been to Kansas City many times, but whenever he returned it seemed to have grown even larger. He decided to simply use a hotel, livery and restaurant near the train station. He had to be back at the station for an eight-fifteen a.m. train.

Lucky for him, the hotel he chose, The Wescott, had its own livery stable and restaurant. He left his horse with someone in front, checked in, went to his room to freshen up, and then to the restaurant for a steak. He was told that when he checked out, his horse would be waiting for him out front, saddled and ready.

The steak was excellent, the vegetables cooked to perfection, and the coffee just the way he liked it. If he had ridden in under normal circumstances, with no other destination in mind, he would have stayed indefinitely. But since he had to leave the next morning, he decided not to try the hotel's bar. He went to his room, read for a short while—Sir Walter Scott's *Ivanhoe*—which he had started once before but never finished. He couldn't remember why, since he was enjoying it so much. He read several chapters, then doused the light and turned in.

***

He woke early enough to have breakfast in the hotel, then checked out. Outside he found the Tobiano, saddled and ready. He rode him to the train, got him situated in the stock car, then found his way to his own seat. Although the trip was a long one, he had chosen not to spend money on a sleeping car. He'd just have to make himself comfortable in his seat.

The car, which could probably accommodate forty people, seemed only half full at that hour. Of course, there was no way of knowing how many more passengers would board between Kansas City and Denver. It was six hundred miles, so there would be a lot of boarding and disembarking.

For the moment, there was plenty of room for him to fold his arms and stretch his legs, but the fact was, he had slept well the night before. He had taken *Ivanhoe* from his saddlebag before putting Toby in the stock car, so he opened it and began reading.

The train stopped several times, allowing passengers to board and disembark. As expected, the car began to fill. An attractive woman in her forties, dressed to travel in a blue dress and matching hat, sat across from him. Upon sitting, she smiled, and he returned it.

Later in the day, a man sat next to her with a drummer's bag, which he kept on his lap. No sooner had the train started moving again when the man began talking to her. Clint could see the man was quite taken with her and was trying, vainly, to attract her attention. Finally, she'd had enough.

"Sir, if you're going to sit there all the way to Denver, I would appreciate it if you would stop talking to me."

The man, a tall, slender man in his late forties, said, "Hey, I was only trying to be neighborly."

"Well," she said, "you've been quite annoying."

"You know, women like you always think they can be bitch—" he started, but Clint stopped him by leaning forward and tapping on his case.

"Hey, friend, take it somewhere else."

"What?" the man asked, looking shocked.

"Go and sit somewhere else," Clint said.

"What the—are you with this lady?" the man asked.

"No, I'm not."

"Then what do you care—"

"The lady is right, my friend," Clint said, "you're annoying, and I'm trying to read. So if you don't move, I'm going to move you."

The man stared at Clint for several seconds before he apparently saw something in his eyes. He grabbed his case, stood, cradled it as if using it as a shield, and left.

Clint sat back.

"That was very gallantly done," the woman said. "Thank you."

"I really was having trouble reading with him rambling on and on," Clint told her.

"So you're telling me you didn't really do it to be gallant?" she said. "I mean, look at what you're reading. You came riding in on your stallion and saved me."

Clint looked at the book in his hands and smiled.

"Okay, maybe Ivanhoe influenced me."

"What's your name?" she asked.

"Clint Adams."

"I'm Laura Jefferies. If you'd allow me to thank you," she said, "we could go to the dining car so I can buy you a drink."

"That sounds good," he said.

He set the book aside, stood and helped her to her feet. She was tall and filled her dress out well in all the right places.

Chapter Nine

In the dining car they decided to sit and not only have drinks, but something to eat. Clint said he would allow her to buy him a drink first, but that he would be paying for the meal.

After a small whiskey each, they looked at the menu. Surprisingly, the kitchen was serving pheasant, so they both ordered it. When the plates came, they stared at their tiny birds.

"The poor things," Laura said.

"At least they're in plum sauce," Clint commented.

She ran her forefinger through a smear of sauce on the plate and stuck it in her mouth.

"It is really good," she admitted, and they started eating.

While they ate, they became acquainted, although Clint kept steering the conversation her way. She designed clothing for women, had a store in Kansas City, and was going to Denver to scout it and see if it would be viable to open another store.

"I think Denver would be perfect for a woman like you," Clint said.

"A woman like me?" she asked. "How do you mean that?"

"Classy, intelligent and, if I may say so, beautiful," he replied.

"You say so," she said. "You're still being gallant. Thank you."

The dining car was starting to fill up.

"Maybe we should go back to our seats and let somebody else sit and eat," she suggested.

"Good idea," he said.

He paid for the dinner, and then followed her through the cars until they reached their seats. There was only darkness outside their windows.

"Seems we have no more scenery to watch until morning," she said. "That means you finally have to talk about yourself."

"We talked," he said.

"You don't think I noticed how you kept turning the conversation back to me?" she said. "You can't get away with that now. Tell me something about Clint Adams. Why are you going to Denver?"

Clint had the distinct feeling that he had met someone to whom his name meant nothing. To his way of thinking, that was not a bad thing. So he didn't want to tell her who he was, and he certainly didn't want to tell her why he was going to Denver.

So he lied.

Sort of.

"I have a friend who lives there," he said, which was true. "And I'm going to visit him." Which was also true, once Roper came home.

"I see," she said. "And what does this friend do?"

"He's a private detective."

"A Pinkerton?" she asked.

"No," Clint said, "the Pinkertons wanted him, but he prefers to be on his own."

"I see," she said. "And you? Are you also a private detective?"

"No, I'm not," he said. "I leave all that kind of work to Tal."

"Tal?"

"His name's Talbot Roper," he said.

"Oh, I see," she said.

"He's very good at his job . . ." he said, and continued to talk about Roper, so that he wouldn't have to talk about himself.

"You seem very impressed with your friend," she said, when he finally wound down.

"Well, yes," Clint said. "I believe he's the very best at what he does."

She nodded.

"And are you the very best at what you do . . . Mr. Gunsmith?"

Chapter Ten

Clint dozed in his seat, comfortable because no one had taken the seat next to him. Across from him, Laura was also dozing, with no one seated next to her. Then, at one point, she opened her eyes and saw that he was also awake.

"I'm getting a stiff neck," she said. "Would you mind if I sit next to you and lean my head on your shoulder?"

"Not at all," he said.

She smiled and shifted seats, then leaned against him. In moments she was asleep, and he was aware of the heat of her body through their clothes. Eventually, he also fell asleep.

When he stirred in the morning, Laura was still asleep on his shoulder. Since they would be in Denver soon, he decided to wake her.

"Laura?"

"Hmm?"

"We're almost there," he said. "I thought you might like to . . . freshen up."

"Yes," she said, sitting up, "yes, I would. Thank you. Excuse me."

She stood and walked off down the aisle to the ladies' lavatory. There was also a men's lavatory for Clint to use. By the time they both returned to their seats, they were refreshed and awake.

"This would've been a much shorter trip without all those stops," Laura observed.

"Unfortunately, there were many people getting on and off," he said.

"I understand they have express trains, now," she said. "Perhaps next time I'll spend the extra money."

"Well," Clint said, "I have to admit I didn't find this trip too unpleasant. I think that had something to do with the company."

"Ah," she said, "gallant to the last stop."

***

When they pulled into Denver's Union Station, Clint helped Laura down from the railroad car.

"I have to get my horse from the stock car," he said.

"Would you be able to recommend a hotel?" she asked.

"Whenever I'm in Denver, I always use the Denver House. Any cab driver will know where that is."

"Well, then," she said, "perhaps I'll see you there."

As they parted away, he thought about the Denver House. He liked the hotel and they treated him well, but it was one of the more expensive places in town. He certainly didn't want Laura to discover that he couldn't stay there because of his money problems. But he could probably afford a couple of days, and maybe he'd be able to get the information he wanted by then.

He collected the Tobiano from the stock car and rode to the Denver House.

***

"How nice to see you again, Mr. Adams," the clerk said. "Same room?"

"Please," Clint said. "I'd appreciate it." He accepted his key. The hotel had its own livery, and Toby was safely tucked away.

"Can we do anything else for you, sir?"

"I recommended the hotel to a lady on the train," Clint said. "I wonder if she checked in?"

"And her name?" the clerk asked, opening the register.

"Laura Jefferies."

"Yes," the clerk said, "Miss Jefferies checked in just a short time ago."

"Ah, good," Clint said. "Thank you."

Clint went to his room, still the most comfortable room of any hotel, he had ever been in. He made use of the indoor plumbing. Refreshed and wearing clean clothes, he headed right for his bank.

***

He had been using the National Bank of Denver for his businesses ever since he started investing. There were a couple of mines, several saloons, a few other, smaller businesses that didn't last. But it was the saloons that brought in most of his money.

Rick Hartman had left him the saloon, Rick's Place, in Mission City, when he died. Clint had two partners running it for him. It had only been a few months, but so far the place was very profitable. Until now . . .

It would be easy for him to send telegrams to the saloons, harder to get a message to his partners in the mines. But first, he wanted to go directly to the bank and speak with the president. Maybe he wouldn't have to go after his partners if the bank president could tell him what happened to his money.

Chapter Eleven

The First Denver was the largest bank Clint had ever been inside. There were more teller's cages and desks than he'd ever seen, high ceilings dotted with gold chandeliers. In order to get to the president of the bank, he had to speak first to a clerk, then to the bank manager, whose name was Hector Baxter.

"I'm sure I can help you, sir," Baxter said.

"You might, at that," Clint said, "but I think this is a matter for the top man."

"I'm afraid our president is a very busy man—"

"Mr. Baxter," Clint said, "I don't want to have to insist. Why don't you tell him I'm here and let him decide if he has the time to see me?"

"Very well. Please wait here."

The manager didn't have his own office, just a desk at the back of the large room. He rose and went to a set of stairs. It was obvious that the president of the bank had an office on the second floor of the two-story bank building.

When Baxter came back down, he said, "Mr. Ingram will see you now. Please follow me."

"Thank you."

4

very tall and thin, with an angular face that ended in a
pointed chin. Baxter, on the other hand, was small and
pudgy, looking more like a banker. Both men were in
their forties.

"Thank you, Baxter," he said in a deep voice.
"That's all."

Baxter withdrew and closed the door.

"Mr. Adams," Ingram said, coming around the desk
to shake hands, "a pleasure. My name is Vincent Ingram. Please, have a seat and tell me what I can do for
you."

"You can tell me what happened to all my money,"
Clint said. "A bank in Kansas told me it's all gone. I said
that can't be possible. I didn't withdraw it."

"Does anyone else have access to your account?"

"Just to make deposits," Clint said.

"Hmm, then perhaps there's been an error some-
place," Ingram said. "Why don't you let me have a look
into the matter and see what I can find out."

"That's what I was hoping for."

46

"All I know at the moment is that you are a longtime depositor, which makes you valuable to us. And I am also aware of your reputation."

"That's good."

"Give me the rest of today," Ingram said, "and come back tomorrow. Hopefully, I'll have some answers for you. Is that satisfactory?"

"It is for now," Clint said. "I can't say about tomorrow."

"Of course," Ingram said. "Shall I have someone show you out?"

"I know the way."

Ingram stood to shake hands again.

"When you return tomorrow just see Baxter, and he'll bring you up."

"Thank you, Mr. Ingram."

Clint rose, left the office and the bank.

***

Clint had two options of what to do next. He could go to the hotel and see if he could find Laura Jefferies, or he could go to Talbot Roper's office and see if he was back from his out- of-town case. He decided to check on Roper first. Usually, his friend had a girl manning his office while he was away, but Clint knocked on the door several times before admitting to himself that no one was there. And the fact that there was mail sitting outside the door was further indication.

Giving up on Roper, he went back to his hotel to see if he could catch Laura.

***

He stopped at the front desk to get Laura's room number. Since the clerk knew him, there was no problem.

"Do you know if she's in her room now?" he asked the clerk.

"I'm sorry, no, sir, I don't," the clerk said.

"Okay, thanks."

He went to the second floor, found her room—down the hall from his—and knocked on the door. He knocked several times, but she wasn't there.

He went back down to the lobby, rather than to his room to read *Ivanhoe*. Instead, he went into the hotel bar, which was doing a scarce business that early in the day.

"Beer," he told the bartender, who he didn't recognize from his other stops in the hotel.

"Comin' up," the bartender said. "Are you a guest?"

"I am."

The bartender nodded, set him up with a beer and didn't ask for a dime. The cost of the drink would be attached to his room when he checked out. The same went for any meals he had in the hotel while he was there.

He decided to just lounge at the bar for a while, with a beer or two.

Chapter Twelve

Halfway through the second beer, he saw Laura Jefferies come to the doorway of the bar. She looked around, spotted him, smiled and walked over.

"Is this a coincidence?" he asked.

"I think not," she said. "The desk clerk told me you were looking for me and where I could find you."

"I'll have to give him a sizeable tip," Clint said. "Would you like a drink?"

"Sure," she said, "I'll just have what you're having."

Clint ordered two more beers.

"Why don't we go to a table," he proposed.

"Lead the way."

He did, to a table in the back, from where he would be able to see the entire room.

"How did your day of scouting for a location go?" he asked.

"It went really well," she said. "I found a couple of places that might be a good fit. I also spoke with other store owners in the area, to see what they had to say about the location."

"That was smart," he commented.

"What about your day?"

"Ah, well," he said, "I don't know that I accomplished anything. I'll probably find that out tomorrow."

"So what will you be doing tonight?"

"Dinner, for one thing," he said. "But I'd prefer not to eat alone."

"Is that an invitation?"

"It is."

"Then I accept," she said. "But I've been walking around all day. I need to freshen up, maybe even have a bath."

"No problem," he said. "Why don't we meet in the lobby at eight?"

"Sounds good." She finished her beer. "Thanks for the drink."

He decided not to walk her to her room. Who knew what might happen. Something was certainly going on between them, or she wouldn't have come looking for him.

As if thinking the same thing she said, "Don't walk me to my door. I'll see you in a little while in the lobby."

"I'll just sit here and finish my beer," he said.

She smiled, stood and left. Clint stood up and walked back to the bar.

"Fresh one?" the bartender asked.

"One more," he said.

"Nice lookin' lady," the barman said, as he set it down. "Knows how to drink beer. Most women don't."

"You're right," Clint said. "Women usually drink wine, or sherry."

"Or champagne," the bartender said. "The working girls drink champagne."

"Right."

The bartender leaned his elbows on the bar.

"So what brings you to Denver?" he asked. "The lady?"

"No," Clint said, "we just happened to meet on the train. I have some business here."

"What kind of business?"

"Banking."

The bartender laughed and stood straight up. He was over six feet, rangy with wide shoulders, probably in his thirties. "You sure don't look like a banker."

"I'm not," Clint said, "but my business is with a bank."

"You gonna rob it?" the bartender asked, and then laughed, again.

"Do I look like a bank robber?" Clint asked.

"Well," the bartender said, "more like a bank robber than a banker."

"That's fair," Clint said. He finished his beer and set the empty on the bar. "Thanks."

"Any time," the bartender said. "Good luck with the lady."

***

As he walked past the front desk the clerk waved frantically.

"Fella just left this for you," the clerk said. "He claimed it was urgent."

"Did you tell him where I was?"

"Yessir," the clerk said, "but he just left it with me and ran out."

Clint took the folded piece of paper and said, "Thank you."

He took it with him to his room, where he unfolded and read it. It was from the bank president, Ingram, and it said he had some information for him, would he come to the bank at seven a.m., before it opened. Clint refolded the message and set it aside. If this message was on the level, the man may have some good news. But he couldn't shake the nagging feeling that something was wrong.

He hadn't told Vincent Ingram, or anyone else at the bank, where he was staying.

Chapter Thirteen

Clint thought about the message while he washed and dressed for dinner with Laura. How did Ingram know where he was staying, and why ask him to come to the bank before opening? It made no sense, unless the president himself was up to something he didn't want his staff to know about. Clint didn't know where the president of the bank lived, so his only option was to go to the bank in the morning and be ready for anything. Ingram was a bank president, for chrissake, would he really try something like killing him, or having him killed? If he was stealing money, maybe.

If Talbot Roper was in town, Clint would've used him as backup, or would have even asked him to locate Ingram's home. But Roper wasn't in town; Clint was on his own.

There was nothing he could do about it now, so he left his room and went downstairs to meet Laura in the lobby. He got there before her and sat in a leather divan against the wall to wait. He was still thinking about his situation when she came down the stairs, wearing a lovely green dress. As she approached him, he stood momentarily forgetting his problems.

"Now I feel bad that we're going to eat here," he told her. "I'd like to take you out and show you off."

"You're sweet," she said, "but eating here is fine with me."

They went to the dining room and got seated. This time Laura ordered a glass of white wine, but Clint stayed with beer. She ordered chicken and Clint stayed with steak.

"Do you ever eat anything other than steak?" she asked.

"Hey," he said, "didn't we both have pheasant on the train?" he reminded her.

"You're right," she said. "I apologize."

"But I do eat a lot of steak," he said. "There are days I have it for breakfast and supper. But I do like to try other things."

"What other kinds of food have you tried?" she asked.

"Well, I've eaten Mexican, Chinese, Japanese, German, uh, oh, I had some gypsy food—"

"Oh," she said interrupting him, "tell me about that . . ."

***

They discussed many things, talking all through dinner and dessert, and then noticing that the waiters were
beginning to stack chairs on the tables for the night.

"I think they're trying to tell us something," he said.

"Yes," she said, "I suppose we should let them close
up."

They stood and went into the lobby, with Clint first
making sure that the meal would appear on his hotel bill,
not hers. He just hoped when he checked out he would
be able to pay it—but that would come later.

"We can have a drink at the bar—" he started, as
they reached the lobby.

"I have a bottle of wine in my room," she said. "If
you don't mind wine?"

"I'll make do," he told her.

They went upstairs and he followed her to her door,
waited while she unlocked it and went in ahead of him.
When he was inside, she closed and locked the door,
then turned to face him.

"Wine?"

"Yes," he said, "but first . . ." He stepped to her, put
his hands on her waist, drew her to him and kissed her.
It went on for some time before they parted, both of
them breathless.

"Well," she said, "I have to say that was worth waiting for."

"How long have I kept you waiting?" he asked.

"I have to admit," she said, "it's been ever since the train."

"Well, I'm sorry I kept you waiting," he said. "I was determined to be a gentleman."

"Can we do away with that idea, now?"

"By all means." He ran his hands over the fabric of her garment. "I like this dress."

She smiled, and he found it lewd and daring.

"Tear it!" she said.

He didn't hesitate. He closed his hands on the dress and pulled. It tore away from her body in shreds as he kept tearing, and eventually it was in tatters all over the floor. She stood there in her frilly underthings, her skin smooth and golden.

"Don't stop now," she said.

Her camisole came off easily, and he tossed it away. Then he snapped the straps of her brassiere and her breasts bobbed free, large and firm, her nipples already hard. The last thing to go was the wisp of silk covering her hips, butt and pussy. He just yanked it with one hand and dropped it.

And she was naked.

She was breathing hard; he could already smell that she was wet between her legs.

"I don't think I'm going to be able to do that to you," she said, "so I think I'll just watch."

She stepped back and folded her arms across her naked breasts.

He undressed while she watched with obvious pleasure.

Chapter Fourteen

When he was naked, he walked to the bed and hung his gunbelt on the bedpost. For a moment he stared at the Schofield as if he'd never seen it before, then remembered where it had come from.

"Something wrong, cowboy?" She came up behind him, reached around and took hold of his hard cock.

"No, Ma'am," he said, "nothing's wrong, at all."

"That's good," she said, pressing herself up against his back. As she stroked his penis, he could feel her breasts and nipples flattened against his back, and her pubic hair on the back of his thighs. She ran her other hand over his chest.

He put his hands behind him and took hold of her butt, then said, "We're not going to get much done in this position."

"Just another minute," she said, into his ear, "I'm kind of enjoying this."

She began to pump his cock faster and faster, until he finally had to turn around to get her to stop before he spewed a load all over the wall.

She laughed as he put his arms around her and dragged her down to the bed.

***

Across town, in a large house located in an expensive neighborhood called Washington Park, Vincent Ingram sat in his den and poured himself another glass of whiskey. He'd been drinking ever since he got home from work, right after Clint Adams left his office.

He had come home and locked himself in his den, trying to figure out what to do. Adams was coming back the next day to find out where his money was, and Ingram didn't know what he was going to tell him.

"Vincent?"

He looked up and saw his wife standing in the door.

"What's going on?" she asked. "You've been in here all evening—and your drunk?"

"I wish I was drunk, Grace," he said. "I wish I was." He showed her his empty glass. "This doesn't seem to be doing the job."

"What is it?" She crossed the room, dressed for bed with a robe over her nightgown. Once she had been a beautiful woman, but the years had taken their toll. He always figured that was all right, because once he'd been a handsome man. Now the weight was falling off him by pounds every day and he knew he looked like a scarecrow.

She crouched down next to his chair and put her hand on his arm. He knew she could feel the difference in him, but he didn't mention the changes in her, and she didn't say a word about him. It was a silent agreement.

"Did something happen at the bank today?" she asked.

"Yes, something did."

"Is it bad?"

"It might just be something I can't fix," he said.

"Well, when will you know?" she asked.

"In the morning," he said. "I'll know in the morning."

"Then stop drinking and come to bed," she said. "If you just sit in here, morning will never come."

He looked at his empty glass and knew she was right. He put it down on the table next to his chair, stood up and walked upstairs to the bedroom with her.

***

Clint spent the next few hours forgetting his problems, thanks to the opulent flesh covering Laura Jefferies. She was extremely receptive to his touch and had the knowing hands and mouth of a woman who enjoyed what she was doing and did it well.

They rolled around the large bed together, changing positions every so often so that he was on top, she was on top—at one point she was on all fours and he was behind her. He slid his cock up between her solid thighs and into her wet pussy.

"Oh, God, yes," she said, and began moving her butt back and forth, matching his rhythm as he fucked her from behind that way. As if she could feel him swelling inside her, she scooted away from him, his cock sliding out of her before he could explode.

She wrestled him down onto his back, shimmied down between his legs and began kissing and rubbing his thighs, his testicles, sliding her tongue up and down his cock, and then taking him fully into her mouth.

She slid her hands beneath him to cup his buttocks and squeezed tightly as she continued to bob her head up and down on him, his cock sliding wetly in, almost out, and then back into her mouth. She didn't ever let him out, though. She took his entire cock down deep into her throat, then let it slide out, all except the head, which she swirled her tongue around before taking him all the way in, again.

Clint felt his release working its way up his thighs and this time, she didn't stop him by squeezing his balls. This time she just let him explode into her mouth like a geyser.

Chapter Fifteen

Clint woke with his legs still entwined with Laura's. It was not an unpleasant experience, but it made it difficult for him to rise without waking her.

"No," she moaned, as he slid out of bed, "don't go."

"I have to," he said. "I have an appointment this morning."

She made a rude sound with her mouth.

"Now, now," he said, "don't you have business today?"

"No," she said, petulantly. "I'm just going to wait here for you to come back."

"That's all right with me," he said. "I should still be back in time for breakfast."

He strapped on his gun, then leaned over and kissed her.

"I thought you were going to a bank," she said.

"I am."

"Then why the gun?"

"A gun is always with me, Laura," Clint said. "Maybe when I come back, I'll explain."

"I'm sorry," she said. "I already know. I was just being stupid."

"There's nothing stupid about you," he assured. "See you in a little while."

***

He was across the street from the bank at five minutes to seven. There was no sign of Mr. Ingram out front, but he did see some movement inside the bank, through the glass doors and windows. Carefully, he crossed the street and approached the front doors. When he knocked a uniformed security guard appeared.

"Not open yet!" the guard yelled through the door.

"I have an appointment with Mr. Ingram," Clint called back. "At seven."

The guard frowned and unlocked the door, but didn't open it all the way, just a crack.

"I seen you here yesterday?" he said. Clint remembered the guard from the day before, a solidly built man in his forties.

"That's right," Clint said. "I saw Mr. Ingram yesterday, and he told me to come back today at seven."

"He knows we don't open til eight," the guard said. "Why's he makin' appointments for seven?"

"I don't know," Clint said. "I only know I'm going to be late."

"Yeah, okay," the guard said, opening the door wide. "Mr. Baxter ain't here. I'll take you to Miss Holmes and she can take you to Mr. Ingram."

"Thanks."

Miss Holmes turned out to be a rather mousy young women who sat at one of the many desks.

"Miss Holmes, can you take this man—"

"Clint Adams," Clint said.

"Can you take Mr. Adams up to Mr. Ingram's office? He has a seven o'clock appointment."

"Of course, John," she said, standing and smiling at Clint. She touched her hair, then adjusted the wire-framed glasses on her pert nose. "Follow me, please."

"Sure."

He followed the young girl up the stairs to the second floor, and down the hall to the doors of Ingram's office. When they entered, the outer office was empty, as it had been the day before.

"Let me tell him that you're here," she said.

"Thank you."

She went to the door of the inner office, knocked and entered. Moments later she came out and said, "He'll be with you in a few minutes. He asked if you'd mind waiting."

"No problem."

He took a seat.

"I have to go back to work," she said.

"Okay," he said. "I'll just wait right here."

She nodded, touched her glasses again, and then went out.

Not even one minute went by when Clint heard the shot. He wasn't sure where it had come from, but his only option seemed to be Ingram's office.

He jumped up and ran to the door, found it locked. He put his shoulder to it, hard, and it popped open. He looked around, and found Mr. Ingram on the floor behind his desk, dead. He crouched over the body to check it. At that point the girl, Miss Holmes, came running in.

"I was almost to the stairs when I heard—" She stopped short when she saw Ingram's body. "Oh my God, what did you do?" she blurted.

"I didn't do a thing," he said. "I never even got to come in—"

But she was through listening. She turned and began running down the hall, yelling at the top of her lungs, "Help! Help! He's killed Mr. Ingram!"

Clint knew he had no choice but to wait for folks to start arriving, including the police.

Chapter Sixteen

The first person to arrive was the guard. He ran into the room aiming his gun. Clint already had his hands up.

"H-hands up," the guard ordered, pointing his gun at Clint.

"My hands are already up."

"W-where's Mr. Ingram?" the guard asked. "Miss Holmes says you killed 'im."

"He's on the floor behind his desk," Clint said. "He's dead; but I didn't kill him. I was sitting in the outer office."

The guard moved around so he could see the body.

"Omigod!" He looked at Clint. "W-what do I do?"

"What's your name?"

"J-John."

"Well, John," Clint said, "take my gun, sit me down, and call the police."

"You'll talk to the police?"

"Of course," Clint said. "I told you, I had an appointment with him. I was in the other office when I heard the shot. That's all I know, and that's what I'll tell them."

"A-and you'll give me your gun? No trouble?"

"No trouble," Clint said. "My hands are raised. Take it from my holster."

The guard moved toward him slowly, then snatched the gun out of Clint's holster and tucked it into his own belt.

"Now John, I'm going to sit down on that couch and wait. Is someone sending for the law?"

"Yes," John said, "one of the tellers ran out."

"Okay," Clint said, walking to the sofa and sitting. "Now we wait. When does Mr. Baxter get here?"

"Usually just before eight."

"Then I guess he'll be in charge of the bank when he arrives."

"Huh? Oh yeah, I guess so."

"John," Clint said, "you're too nervous. You're going to shoot me by accident. I didn't kill Mr. Ingram."

"H-how do I know that?"

"Smell my gun," Clint said. "It hasn't been fired."

John took the gun from his belt, sniffed it and put it back.

"See? Now, just try to relax."

The guard took a deep breath and let it out slowly.

"There you go. Now listen, I was in the outer office. So how does somebody shoot Ingram and then get out of here?"

"I—I dunno," John said.

"Come on, John," Clint said. "Sit down. It may take the police a while to get here."

John looked around, saw another chair and sat in it, keeping his gun on Clint.

"You ever been in here before, John?"

"No, never."

"So then you don't know if there's another door."

John looked around.

"I don't see another door," he said.

"A hidden door."

"I don't know nothing about that."

"Well," Clint said, "maybe the police can find out."

When the police arrived, there were two men in uniforms, neither of which looked old enough to have seen many dead men, before. They looked at the body and turned to the guard.

"Is this the man who shot him?"

"He says no," the guard said. "He says he was sittin' in the outer office when he heard the shot."

"Is that his gun?" one policeman asked, pointing to John's belt.

"Yes."

"Let me have it."

John handed it over. The policeman smelled it, then looked at his partner.

"Ain't been fired," he said.

"I don't care," the other one said. "We should hand-cuff him until our boss gets here."

"He's right," Clint said, holding out his wrists.

"He's cooperatin'," John told them.

"Okay, then," one of the policemen said. He stepped toward Clint while the other man covered him, snapped his handcuffs on their suspect.

"Now what?" the policeman with the gun asked.

"Now we wait for your boss," Clint said, "but while we're here, maybe you might want to try and figure out how somebody shot that man, and then got out of this room without going past me."

"What?" one policeman said.

"You sayin' there's some sort of secret door in here?" the other one asked.

"Either that or a trap door in the floor," Clint said. "That's the only explanation I can come up with."

The two policemen and the guard all stared at him.

"There's another explanation," the first policeman, the one who had handcuffed him, offered.

"And what's that?" Clint asked.

"That you killed him."

Chapter Seventeen

Clint knew he should sit quietly and wait for the two policemen's boss. There was no point trying to convince them of anything. They felt they had him dead to rights. He needed someone with a brain to come and take over the situation.

So he sat quietly while the two policemen and the guard tried to keep people from crowding into the room. Apparently, nobody had thought to keep the bank closed.

Finally, a man in a suit entered and looked around. He was short and stocky, sucking on a big cigar. Clint was sure this was the boss they had all been waiting for.

He went over to the two uniformed men, first. They talked, pointed at Clint, and then the newcomer took Clint's gun from the uniformed man and smelled it. Then he turned and walked over to Clint.

"Here's your gun back, Mr. Adams," he said, holding it out.

Clint showed the man his handcuffed hands.

"Take these cuffs off!" the man yelled.

One of the policemen came over and removed the handcuffs from Clint's wrists.

"Thanks," Clint said, rubbing his wrists.

"Tell me what you told them," the man said. "I'll listen."

"Who are you?" Clint asked.

"Oh, sorry," the man said. "I'm Lieutenant Earl Norman. This will be my case."

"Okay," Clint said, "I'll tell you everything I know, and everything I told your two men."

True to his word, the Lieutenant listened to everything Clint had to say. When Clint was done, the Lieutenant turned to his two men.

"Find me a secret way out of this room," he said. "In the wall, or the floor."

"Lieutenant, you're believin' him—"

"Every word," the man said. "His gun hasn't been fired. Start lookin'."

"Yes, sir."

Norman looked at Clint.

"What brought you here to see him?"

On one hand, Clint didn't see any reason not to tell the truth. On the other hand, it might be seen as a motive for murder.

"When I'm going to use a bank, I like to make a thorough investigation of it. Talking to the president seemed the best way to do that."

"So it's just a coincidence that you were here when he got shot?"

"Looks like it."

"I guess you're going to have to talk to somebody else," Norman said.

"Baxter," Clint said.

"Who's that?"

"The bank manager," Clint said.

Norman turned and looked at the guard.

"Is he here yet?"

"Yessir," the guard said. "He's downstairs."

"Bring him up here," the Lieutenant said. "And the girl who heard the shot."

"Yessir."

"Do you need me to stay around any longer?" Clint asked.

"If you don't mind," the man said.

"No problem."

While they waited for the manager, the Lieutenant watched as his men searched the room. Eventually, the guard came in with both the manager, Baxter, and the girl, Miss Holmes.

"You're the bank manager?" Norman asked.

"Y-yes sir," the smaller man said. "Tom Baxter."

"Mr. Baxter, your president is dead," the Lieutenant said. "Does that mean you're now in charge?"

"No sir," Baxter said. "That would be the vice-president, Mr. Cromartie."

"And where is Mr. Cromartie now?"

"I don't know, sir."

"Is he in the building?"

"No, sir," Baxter said, "he didn't come in today."

"Why not?"

"I don't know that."

"Mr. Baxter," Norman said, "get me Mr. Cromartie's home address."

"Yes, sir."

He turned to the girl as Baxter left the office.

"Where were you when you heard the shot?" he asked.

"I was down the hall," she said, "almost to the stairs."

"What did you do?"

"I froze," she said. "I was afraid . . . but then I ran back here, and I saw . . . him leaning over Mr. Ingram." She pointed to Clint.

"And where did you leave Mr. Adams?"

"In the outer office," she said.

"And you didn't see anyone else?"

"No, sir."

"All right," he said, "you can go."

Miss Holmes left the office. Norman started to turn toward Clint, but then one of his men said, "Well, I'll be a sonofabitch."

Chapter Eighteen

"What've you got?" Norman asked.

"You gotta see this, Lieutenant," one man said.

Norman and Clint walked over to where the policeman was standing.

"The whole desk moves," he said. "There's a switch here, and . . ." He activated the switch, and the desk slid aside, revealing a stairway in the floor.

"Tunnels?" Clint asked.

"There are tunnels underneath the city," Norman said. "Most of them haven't been used for years. This bank president must've found one. Maybe he used it to go in and out so nobody would see him."

"That means the killer had to know it was here," Clint said, "and that he'd be able to use it to get in and out."

"Somebody who knows the bank," Norman said. "Like the vice-president of the bank."

At that moment Baxter walked in and his eyes went wide when he saw the stairway.

"You got that address for me?" Norman asked.

"Yessir." Baxter held out a piece of paper.

"All right, thanks," Norman said. He looked at the two policemen. "You guys are coming with me."

"Down there?" one of them asked.

"Yes, down there."

"You mind if I come along?" Clint asked.

"Actually, I do," Norman said. "This is a police matter, Mr. Adams." He looked at the manager. "Mr. Baxter, in the absence of your president and vice-president, maybe you can help Mr. Adams with his business."

"Yessir," Baxter said. "I'll certainly try."

"Thanks for your cooperation, Adams," Norman said. "You can go."

"Would you please follow me to my desk, Mr. Adams?" Baxter asked.

"Sure," Clint said, "why not?"

***

Clint would much rather have gone down into the tunnel with the police, but that would have just been out of curiosity. It wouldn't solve his problem. He hoped maybe Baxter would.

"Oh dear," Baxter said, when Clint told him what had brought him to the bank. "All of it?"

"Every penny, or so I've been told."

"Let me check on this," Baxter said.

He left Clint alone at his desk for about fifteen minutes. Miss Holmes was two desks away, and Clint kept catching her watching him.

Baxter returned, carrying a file.

"I'm sorry, Mr. Adams," he said, "but according to our file, sir, uh, you withdrew the money, yourself."

"That's just not true," Clint said. "Where does it say I did that?"

"Um . . ." Baxter read the file. ". . . and bank in Sacramento."

"Sacramento?" Clint said. "I haven't even been to Sacramento in . . . I don't know how long. What bank does it say I did that at?"

"It says Sacramento Savings and Loan."

"I've never been to that bank." He sat back in his chair and momentarily fumed before speaking again. "How do I find out who withdrew this money?"

"Well, if you go to the bank where it was withdrawn they might be able to, uh, remember."

"In Sacramento."

Baxter nodded.

"How is this possible, Mr. Baxter?" Clint asked. "Doesn't someone withdrawing that much money have to show some sort of identification?"

"In some banks, in some states, yes," Baxter said. "I don't know about Sacramento."

Clint stood up, preparing to leave, but then stopped and turned back.

"I understand some states have implemented insurance for their depositors."

"Yes, sir, I've heard something about that," Baxter said. "I believe that is the case in New York, Vermont, Indiana, Michigan . . . uh . . .oh yes, Ohio and Iowa."

"Well, then," Clint said, "I guess if and when I get my money back, I'd better go to one of those places and deposit it."

"Oh, sir, I hope you won't—"

This time he turned and left.

***

Outside the bank Clint stopped and stared at the building. He wondered where the tunnel from the president's office led. He also wondered where the police were at that moment. Were they still down there, or had they found where it led to? And where could that be?

Chapter Nineteen

Clint now had the location of the bank where his money had been withdrawn. Now he had to get to Sacramento, with his finances once again waning. Once he paid his bill at the Denver House he was going to be in trouble.

The murder of the bank president was interesting, but did it have anything to do with his money? Or was it a coincidence that somebody chose that moment to kill the man?

Once again Clint wished his friend, Tal Roper, was in town. Not only could Roper look into the murder, but he could probably loan Clint enough money to get to Sacramento. Roper was one of the few people he would have asked for a loan, along with Bat Masterson and Luke Short—if he knew where they were.

Then something occurred to him. Since the bank had allowed his funds to be withdrawn by somebody other than him, why shouldn't they finance his trip to Sacramento?

All these thoughts went through his head while he was standing outside the bank, so he went right back inside to talk to Baxter again.

***

"A loan?" Baxter said, nervously.

"That's right," Clint said. "I need to go to Sacramento to find out what happened to my money. You allowed the withdrawal, but it physically happened there."

"Well—"

"It's only fair," Clint went on, cutting him off, "that your bank loan me the money to do it."

Baxter stared at him from behind his wire-frame glasses, his eyes watery.

"What's wrong?" Clint asked.

"This is normally something I would take up with the president or vice-president of the bank."

"Well, then we're in luck," Clint said.

"We are?"

"Sure," Clint said, "they're not here, so you get to make a decision."

"Mr. Adams—"

"And I would sure like you to make one that wouldn't upset me, Mr. Baxter," Clint added.

***

He left the bank with the loan money in his pocket. It would be enough to go to Sacramento, get a hotel for a few days, and find his money. Thankfully, Baxter hadn't had the spine to turn him down.

This also gave him plenty of funds to buy Laura dinner that night, before telling her that he was leaving town the next day. Not wanting to waste any time getting to Sacramento, he went to Union Station and bought his ticket.

***

When Clint got back to his hotel room Laura was gone, leaving behind her scent on his sheets. He really hadn't expected her to wait. After all, he had been gone longer than he said he would be. She had probably gone to breakfast alone, which reminded him that he hadn't eaten, so he went back down to the lobby, and into the dining room.

Eating a late breakfast alone he decided to be leisurely about it. He ordered steak-and-eggs, and a basket of hot biscuits. There was no reason to rush his meal; he had nothing to do until he caught his train tomorrow morning. He had inquired at Union Station about a train that day, but there wasn't one.

So he told the waiter to bring him the biggest steak in the kitchen, and took his time eating it . . .

***

Lieutenant Earl Norman entered his chief's office.

"Close the door," Chief Novak snapped.

Novak was new to Denver, having been hired after leaving his job in New York with the New York City police. At sixty, he was still hard-edged and tough.

"Siddown," he said.

Norman obeyed.

"Tell me about this bank president thing."

Norman explained the situation to him, ending with him and the two officers going through the tunnel and coming out three blocks away in the basement of an abandoned warehouse.

"And why isn't Clint Adams in a cell?" Novak asked.

"Because he didn't do it," Norman said. "In fact, he didn't do a thing. He was just waiting there to see the bank president."

"You mean to tell me a man is shot and it's a coincidence that a renown gunman happens to be present?"

"That's what I'm telling you, sir," Norman said. "His gun hadn't been fired, and he had no motive. He had just met the man briefly the day before."

"You better be right about this, Norman," the chief said. "Just make sure he doesn't leave town until you find the killers."

"Yes, sir, Norman said. "I will do that."

"That's all," Novak said, and Norman left the office.

Chapter Twenty

When Clint came out of the dining room, he saw the policeman, Lieutenant Norman, standing in the lobby. He walked over to him.

"Mr. Adams," the man greeted.

"Lieutenant."

"I saw you eating breakfast and decided not to interrupt you."

"I appreciate that."

"Can we talk?"

"Sure," Clint said. "Too early for a drink?"

"Never."

They went into the bar together and Clint ordered two beers.

"Comin' up, Mr. Adams," the bartender said.

When they got their beers, Clint turned to the lieutenant and asked, "You want to sit?"

"I guess we should."

The bar was empty, not one other customer. Still, Clint walked them to a back table.

"You're a careful man," Norman said.

"That's how I stay alive." Clint sipped his beer. "What can I do for you?"

"We followed that tunnel for a few blocks before it came out in a warehouse," Norman said. "After that there was no trail."

"What about the vice-president? Cromartie?"

"We haven't found him," Norman said. "He wasn't home."

"Think he's running?" Clint asked.

"Or dead, somewhere."

"So what's going on at that bank to make somebody kill the president and maybe the vice president."

"That's what I was going to ask you."

"How would I know?"

"Let me put this another way," Norman said. "What exactly were you doing at the bank?"

Clint studied the man over the rim of his beer mug and decided to tell him the truth.

"Somebody emptied my bank account," Clint said. "I'm trying to find out who."

"What did Ingram tell you?"

"I saw him yesterday," Clint said. "He told me he'd look into it, and that I should come back at seven this morning."

"So you were there when he got killed."

"I don't think that was his plan," Clint said.

"Probably not. So what are you going to do now?"

"Baxter gave me a lead," Clint said. "I'm going to look into it."

"Where?"

"Sacramento," Clint said. "Seems that's where the bank is, where my money was withdrawn."

"Crap," Norman said.

"What is it?"

"I've got this chief who wants me to wrap this murder up quick," Norman said. "He told me to see that you don't leave town."

"Does he think I did it?"

"He just wants to make sure you didn't before we let you go," the lieutenant said.

"Well," Clint said, "I don't want to make things harder for you . . . how long do you think it'll take?"

"I don't know," Norman said, honestly. "I've still got to find that vice-president. I don't have any other leads."

"What about the president's house?"

"We went through it, didn't find anything," Norman said.

"Lieutenant, I've got to find out who took my money and get it back before it's all gone. I've got to go to Sacramento, but like I said, I don't want to cause you trouble."

"My chief's a tough one," Norman said, "Came here from New York."

"How long have you been here?"

"A few months," Norman said. "I got hired just before he arrived. I guess I'm lucky he kept me on."

"Do you know Talbot Roper?"

"The private detective?" Norman said. "Yeah, sure, we've already crossed paths on a couple of cases. You know him?"

"He's a friend of mine."

"Can he vouch for you?" the policeman asked.

"If he was in town, he would," Clint said.

Norman drank some of his beer, and Clint could see the man's mind working.

"Look," the lieutenant said, "I know your reputation; I know you're the Gunsmith. From everything I've heard about you, you're a man of your word."

"That's true."

"If you tell me you didn't kill Ingram, I'll believe you."

"I didn't kill him."

"You know, the money thing could be looked at as a motive," Norman said.

"I didn't kill him."

"Okay," Norman said, "do you know who did? Or why?"

"Not a clue," Clint said. "I'm only looking for my money."

"And you're going to Sacramento."

"Yes."

"I could arrest you to stop you," Norman said.

"You could. Or you could talk to Deputy Marshal Custis Long. He'll vouch for me."

"I know Long," Norman said. "Is he a friend of yours?"

"Not exactly," Clint said, "but like I said, he'll vouch for me. If he doesn't, you can pick me up at Union Station tomorrow morning."

"Okay," Norman said. "You're lucky I don't like my chief. I'll check with the deputy—but do me a favor."

"What's that?"

"When you get to Sacramento, drop me a telegram and let me know where you are," Norman said. "In case I need to get in touch with you."

"I can do that," Clint said. "Thanks for not taking me in now."

"I don't think you killed Ingram," Norman said, "and I believe you didn't know him. It wouldn't do any good to put you in a cell." The lieutenant stood up. "Have a nice trip. I hope you find your money."

"I hope so, too," Clint said.

Chapter Twenty-One

Clint spent the night with Laura, then left her asleep in his bed to go to Union Station. He got the Tobiano settled in the stock car, then headed for the passenger car. Along the way he kept an eye out for Lieutenant Norman. If Marshal Long didn't vouch for him, the policeman would be there to take him in. He would then have to decide if he was going to let him do that. Luckily, it wasn't necessary. Norman didn't show up. Clint got on the train to Sacramento.

***

He kept to himself the whole way. There was a lovely woman in the same car who kept looking over at him, but he decided not to act on it. Not this time . . .

In Sacramento he disembarked, claimed the Tobiano, then rode to a nearby hotel. It wasn't the same class as the Denver House, but it wasn't a flophouse, either. It was called The Rialto Hotel. It would do. Once he checked in, he took Toby to the nearest livery stable. Then he set about to locate the Sacramento Savings and Loan.

"Oh, yes sir," the desk clerk said. "That bank is on Sutter Street."

"Thanks."

"There are banks closer to here, sir," the clerk told him.

"That's okay," Clint said. "I want that one."

It was early enough to go and check it out, so he turned and left the hotel.

***

When he got to the bank he stopped outside. It was larger than most banks he had been to, but smaller than the one in Denver. The building was one-story, made of brick. There was plenty of foot traffic, as well as carts and buggies and wagons going by. He went inside and told the teller he needed to talk to someone about a withdrawal.

"Are you a depositor with us, sir?" the young clerk asked.

"The withdrawal has already been made," Clint said. "I need to know who made it."

"Oh, well, sir, we're not allowed to give out that information."

"Look, the account was mine," Clint said, "but I didn't make the withdrawal. Somebody else cleaned out my account. Now, who do I talk to?"

"Oh," the teller said, "that would be Mr. York, the bank manager."

"No president, no vice-president?" Clint asked.

"Nossir, just the manager."

"Get him!"

"Y-yessir."

The clerk moved away from his cage to a door and knocked, nervously. Clint looked around the interior of the bank. There were another two cages, and several desks. All but one were occupied. From where he stood, he could see a large bank safe against a back wall. When the teller reappeared, he still seemed very nervous.

"You can g-go in, sir," he said.

"Thank you."

As he entered, a man behind a smaller, neat desk stood and greeted him.

"Good-afternoon," he said. "I'm Lionel Packer the bank manager. Jeffery tells me you're missing some money from your account?"

"Not some," Clint said, "*all*."

"Please. Have a seat, Mr. . . .?"

"Adams," he said, "Clint Adams."

"Mr. Adams," Packer repeated, obviously recognizing the name. "Please, tell me exactly what your problem is."

"You gave away all my money," Clint said.

Chapter Twenty-Two

"I beg your pardon?" Packer said, frowning.

"Someone came in here last month and withdrew all my money," Clint said.

"Are—were you a depositor, here?"

"Well, technically, the National Bank of Denver. But they told me someone came in here and got my money. Can you tell me how that could happen?"

"We have a connection to the Denver bank," Packer said. "If someone comes in here to make a withdrawal, we have a telegraph key. We contact the bank in Denver, and if they okay the transaction, it goes through."

"So you're telling me it was their fault, and they're telling me it was your fault. Meanwhile, where's my money?"

"Why don't you give me some time to look into this—"

"That's what they told me in Denver," Clint said, "and then the bank president got murdered."

"What? Mr. Ingram is dead?"

"Shot. And the vice-president is missing."

"My word."

"So, if you don't mind, I'll wait right here while you look into this mess."

Packer blinked several times before he said, "Uh, very well, let me see what I can do." Then he left the office.

Moments later a young lady entered.

"Mr. Adams? Mr. Packer asked me to see if you would like some coffee."

"Yes," he said, "I would. Black and strong."

"I'll be right back."

She left and returned quickly with a cup.

"Here you go," she said, handing him the coffee. She was young, blonde, and pretty.

"What's your name?"

"Angela."

"Thank you, Angela."

A few years ago he would have talked to her further, but these days he was leaving the young ones alone.

"You're welcome," she said, but didn't leave.

"Something else?" he asked.

"Well . . . are you the Gunsmith?" she asked. "That Clint Adams?"

"Yes," he said, "I'm that Clint Adams."

"I didn't know we had such a famous depositor," she said.

"Well," he said, "you may not, after today."

"I hope that's not the case," she said. "I'll check back later to see if you want more coffee."

"Thanks."

She left him alone in the office. He would have used the time to his advantage, to search if he had known what to search for. As it was, he simply sat there, sipping and waiting.

It was about another fifteen minutes before the manager, Packer, returned, carrying a file.

"Well, it seems you're correct," he said. "Someone did come in and withdraw all your funds, but we were under the impression that it was, uh, you."

"Well, it wasn't," Clint said. "I haven't been in Sacramento for some time."

"This is terrible," Packer said, "terrible. I don't know what to tell you."

"What about the teller that handled the withdrawal?" Clint asked.

"Yes, yes," Packer said, looking at the file, "that would be our Mr. Culpepper."

"Can we get him in here and see what he remembers?"

"Of course, of course," Packer said. He went to the door, opened it and said, "Angela, would you ask Mr. Culpepper to come in here, please?"

Clint heard a muffled, "Yes, sir."

Packer returned to his desk.

"I don't know how this could have happened," he said. "We usually make sure we're giving the money to the right person."

"Well," Clint said, "let's find out what Culpepper has to say for himself."

There was a knock on the door, and then a timid looking man in his thirties stuck his head in.

"Mr. Packer, you wanted me?"

"Yes, Culpepper, come in."

The teller came in, closed the door, and then stood nervously.

"Culpepper, this gentleman is Clint Adams," Packer said.

"How do you do, sir?" the teller said.

"Not good," Clint said.

"I'm sorry to hear that."

"Culpepper, have you ever seen this man before?"

The teller studied Clint for a few moments, then said, "No, sir, I don't believe so."

"Well, last month you apparently gave all of Mr. Adams' money to the wrong person."

"Sir?" Culpepper said, frowning. "Oh, wait, you mean the Gunsmith?"

"Yes, Culpepper, I mean the Gunsmith."

"Well, sir, this man isn't the Gunsmith," Culpepper said.

"I'm not?" Clint asked.

"No, sir," Culpepper said, "the Gunsmith came in last month and withdrew all his money."

"And you're sure it was the Gunsmith?" Packer asked.

"Well, yes, sir," Culpepper said. "I wouldn't have given him the money if I wasn't sure."

"Well then," Clint said, "who am I?"

Culpepper looked at Clint and said, "I have no idea, sir."

Chapter Twenty-Three

Clint took some papers out of his pocket and handed them across the desk to Packer. They were letters and contracts he kept in his saddlebags. Packer looked them all over, his face growing pale.

"Culpepper," he said, "this man is Clint Adams, the Gunsmith."

"Sir," Culpepper said, "the man who came in was wearing a gun and, in no uncertain terms, said he was Clint Adams, and he wanted all his money."

"And what did he show you to prove who he was?" Clint asked.

"Well . . ."

"Nothing, right?"

"Well . . ."

"He scared you, didn't he?" Clint asked.

"Um, well, yes," Culpepper said.

"Culpepper," Packer said, "this is a horrible, horrible error on your part."

"Y-yes, sir."

"Tell me, Mr. Culpepper," Clint said, "what did the man look like, other than his gun?"

"Well . . . I kept looking at his gun . . ."

"Had you ever seen him before?"

"Oh, no, sir."

"And have you seen him since?"

"No, sir."

"You've got to think about this hard, Culpepper," Clint said. "What did he look like?"

"Well sir, he was big, a mean looking man, um, in his forties, I think. Sort of dressed like you . . ."

"That's it?" Clint asked.

"I'm sorry, sir."

Clint wasn't sure if the teller was talking to him, or his boss.

"Did he say anything that could tell us where he went, or where he was staying at the time?" Clint asked.

If Packer and Culpepper couldn't come up with more than they had already given him, he wasn't getting his money back any time soon.

"N-no, sir."

Clint looked at Packer.

"All right, Culpepper," Packer said, "that'll be all, for now. I'll talk to you again later."

"Am I going to get fired, sir?"

"Later, Culpepper," Packer said.

"Yes, sir."

The teller left the office. Packer passed Clint's papers back to him.

"I don't suppose your bank is one of those that has insurance?" Clint asked.

"I'm afraid not, sir."

"So what are we going to do about this, Mr. Packer?" Clint asked.

"To tell you the truth, sir, I don't know," Packer said. "I'll have to take it up with my superiors."

"So you want me to come back—when? Tomorrow?"

"Mmmm, I can't say for sure, sir," Packer said. "I'll have to contact them . . . can you tell me what hotel you're staying at?"

"The Rialto."

"I could send you a message when I have something to, uh, tell you."

"And can you guarantee me you won't get killed while I'm waiting?"

Packer looked shocked.

"I certainly hope not!"

"All right, Mr. Packer," Clint said, standing up. "I'll wait to hear from you."

"As soon as I can, sir," Packer said.

Clint left the manager's office, exchanged looks with Culpepper, who was back behind his cage, and then left the bank.

As he stepped outside, he saw a small café across the street, and got an idea. With nothing else to do, he decided to wait til the bank closed, and then follow somebody home. Maybe Packer, maybe Culpepper. He would take the time to decide which over a cup of coffee and a piece of pie.

***

It was five-oh-five when employees began to leave the bank. He saw Angela leave and walk down the street with another woman. Others came out, and then Culpepper appeared, walking by himself. Packer was still inside. As the manager, he was probably the last to leave,

Since it was Culpepper who gave away his money, Clint decided to follow the teller and see where he led him. It was certainly possible that the teller had been in on the theft of his money. With no other options at the moment, why not give this a try?

He paid his bill, left the café, and followed Culpepper at a safe distance.

Chapter Twenty-Four

Culpepper did not go straight home. Instead, he stopped in a restaurant, apparently to have dinner. Luckily, there was another restaurant across the street, smaller and not as busy. Clint got a table by the window, something he usually avoided, but he didn't really expect anyone in Sacramento to take a shot at him through the window.

He ordered chicken, an easy meal to eat, while keeping his eyes on the restaurant across the street. He didn't want to be sawing away at a steak and miss the teller coming out.

He finished eating and ordered a coffee, but before it came, Culpepper appeared at the door across the street. Hurriedly, Clint dropped money on the table and left. Once again, he followed Culpepper at a safe distance.

This time the teller went into a building where it looked like he might have a room above a candle shop. He decided to try to find out. He entered the shop, looked around, grabbed a candle and went to the counter, where an attractive woman looked at him, somewhat amused.

"You don't look the type," she said.

"What type?" he asked.

"The candle type," she said. "Is this for your wife?"

"I don't have a wife."

"Your sweetheart, then?"

"Sorry, don't have one of those, either."

"So you're buying this candle for yourself?"

"Should I lie, or tell you the truth?"

"I like the truth," she told him.

"I followed a man here and I think he went upstairs. Does somebody live there?"

"Mr. Culpepper," she said, nodding. "Is that who you followed?"

"That's him," Clint said.

"Why?" she asked. "He seems so harmless."

"That's what I'm trying to find out," he said. "Do you know if he has any friends?"

"Doesn't everybody?" she asked.

"Does he get many visitors?"

"Not that I notice," she said. "Do you still want the candle?"

"I'll take two," he said.

Wrapping the candles she asked, "What did he do?"

"That's also what I'm trying to find out," he said.

"You know," she said, "I'm closing after this sale."

"You are?"

She nodded.

"If you want to pump me for some more information," she said, "I wouldn't mind a meal."

Even though he had just eaten, it had been a light meal, so he said, "I'd be happy to buy you dinner."

"Then I'll tell you all I know," she said. "Wait for me outside?"

"I'll do that."

"Hey," she said, as he turned to leave, "your candles."

"Right." He took the candles from her and went outside.

While waiting he tried to open the other door, found it locked. Then the door to the store opened and the woman came out, taking a moment to lock up behind her.

"What's your name?" she asked.

"Clint."

"I'm Amy." She slipped her arm inside his left one. "Shall we go?"

"I'm all yours," he said.

***

Amy took him to a restaurant called The Blossom, a few blocks away.

"Shall I order for both of us?" she asked, when they sat.

"Why not?" he said. "I'm in your hands."

"You know, I've never done this before," she said, after she ordered.

"Eaten with a man?"

"Not with one I just met," she said.

"Why me, then?" he asked.

"I find you interesting," she answered.

"Because I bought some candles?"

"Because you told me the truth when I called you on it. And because you still bought the candles."

"All right, then," he said, "what else can you tell me about Culpepper?"

"He's polite, quiet, he never comes into my store—"

"Then how do you know he's quiet and polite?"

"Occasionally we see each other on the street, in front of the building. He says hello, but that's all." She leaned on the table. "So what did he do?"

Since he'd been truthful so far, he decided to keep going.

"He gave away all my money."

"What?"

He told her the story, and she listened in rapt attention.

"I knew he worked in a bank," she said. "Do you really think he was aware of what he was doing?"

"I don't know what to think," he said, "but rather than just wait at my hotel, I thought I'd follow him."

"And you met me?"

"See?" he said, as the waiter came with their food, "no harm done."

Chapter Twenty-Five

Amy had ordered beef stew for both of them, and Clint found it delicious. He also found her company pleasant. She told him how she had married young, but her husband died, and she had not remarried. Now she was in her thirties, had her own business, and felt she was doing fine.

"And you?" she asked. "Were you a rich man before you lost your money?"

"Not rich," he said, "and it's not lost, yet. I still have hopes of getting it back."

"So it would be very helpful to you if Culpepper was one of the thieves."

"Yes, it would."

"What did you do to get your money?"

"Investments," he said. "Saloons, restaurants, some mines."

"Gold mines?"

"I have a piece of a gold mine, yes," he said.

"So you could end up rich."

"I doubt it," he said, "but I guess it's possible."

"What's your full name?"

"Clint Adams."

She sat back in her chair.

"The Clint Adams I've heard of is a gunman called the Gunsmith," she said. "Are you . . .?

"I am that Clint Adams," he said. "I don't like to think of myself as a gunman."

"I'm sorry—"

"That's okay," he said. "That *is* what the newspapers call me."

"My full name is Amy Locane," she said. "I'm just a candle lady."

"It's a beautiful little store," he said. "It smells nice—or that maybe you."

"Probably both," she said, with a laugh.

They continued to eat and get acquainted.

***

After they finished and left the restaurant she said, "I live walking distance from here."

"I'll walk you home," he said. "Why don't you live upstairs from your shop?"

"Culpepper was already living there when I opened last year," she told him.

"Does anyone else live there?"

"No," she said, "there's only one tenant."

They turned down a street that was lined with small, one-story houses.

"I'm here," she said.

"Nice little house," he observed.

"It's the one thing my husband left me when he died," she said.

"You mentioned that before," Clint said. "How old were you when he died?"

"Twenty-two," she said. "We were only married for five years."

"And how did he die?"

"Fever," she said. "The doctors weren't even sure what caused it, but there was nothing they could do about it. He died during the night while I was by his bed."

"That must've been terrible for someone so young."

"It was," she said. "It took me a while to get my feet under me, again."

He walked her to her door, which she unlocked and then turned to face him.

"Come inside?" she asked.

"I'd like to, but I should probably get back to my hotel—" he started, and she cut him off.

"You know what I'm asking you, don't you?"

"I think so . . ."

"If I tell you something that would help you, would you come inside with me?"

"Amy—"

"It's really going to help you," she said. "I'll trade it for a little more of your time."

"What is it?" he asked.

"I happen to have a key to Culpepper's place."

"How'd you manage that?"

"The owner of the building thought I should have it in case of an emergency. You know, like a fire."

"And does Culpepper have a key to your place?"

"No."

He gave that some thought.

"Tomorrow morning, after he goes to work, I could let you into his place," she added.

If he had the opportunity to search Culpepper's home, he might find something useful. Or he might be able to cross the man off the list of thieves. But it sure would have been easier to get Clint's money if there was somebody on the inside.

"I think you have a deal," he said.

She smiled, took his hand and led him inside . . .

Chapter Twenty-Six

Amy tugged Clint all the way through the darkened interior of the house to her bedroom.

"Please don't think badly of me," she said, "but when you walked into my shop, I wanted to take all my clothes off—and yours."

"Well," he said, reaching for her, "let's start with yours."

He kissed her while he undid the buttons on the back of her dress. The skin of her back was like silk. He peeled the dress down to her waist, kissed her neck and the upper slopes of her large breasts. The dress dropped to her ankles and she stepped out of it. Clint peeled off her underthings, and she stood before him gloriously naked.

"Well," she said, huskily, "there's one of my wishes."

He undid his gunbelt and set it nearby, then slowly undressed while she watched. The boots took the longest, but once he got them tugged off, getting rid of the rest of his clothes was easy.

They came together, her hot flesh pressed against his, his hard cock trapped between them, her breasts flattened against his chest.

He ran his hands down her smooth back until he was clutching her ass, which was more than a handful. She writhed in his grasp, rubbing up against him, the friction making his hard cock even harder.

She backed away for a moment, so she could reach between them and take hold of his penis. Holding it tightly, she pulled him to the bed and pushed him down onto his back. That done, she crawled on top of him and began to kiss him everywhere. She worked her way from his neck to his chest to his belly, until she had her face pressed to his hot erection. She rubbed it on her cheeks, kissed it, licked the length of it, wetting it thoroughly before taking it into her mouth. She sucked him avidly, and he strained, lifting his butt off the bed, trying to control the urge to just explode. She made a sound like "Mmmmm," as if she was sucking on something very sweet.

Finally, just when he thought he couldn't take any more, she released him from her mouth, crawled atop him again and took him into her hot vagina.

She rode him hard until he didn't have a choice but to simply erupt inside of her . . .

***

Later they rolled on the bed together until he had her on the bottom, and he could return the favor. He got down between her thighs, spread them widely, started by kissing their soft, smooth flesh. Then he centered his attention on her pussy, which was soaking wet. He licked up her liquid, so that she was now wet with his saliva. He drove his tongue into her pussy, causing her to gasp and grab for his head. Then he started working his tongue and she had no choice but to grab a handful of sheet on either side of her, her body going taut, until she exploded into uncontrollable spasms.

He didn't wait for the waves to subside. He simply got between her thighs on his knees, drove his cock into her while she was still in the throes of her passion. He fucked her hard, because she not only craved it but called out for it.

"Yes," she shouted, "harder, faster, yes, like that . . ."

They were both making plenty of noise, and if they had been in his hotel room, he might have worried about it. But they were in her house, so they could be as loud as they wanted.

When he finally let loose inside of her, it was a competition to see which one of them shouted the loudest . . .

***

"What's the name of your shop?" he asked.

"You didn't notice?" she asked. "On the window it says 'The Candle Lady.' "

"Well," he said, placing his hand on her thigh, "this isn't what most people would expect from a candle lady."

"You know," she said, "every candle needs a flame, and I have a fire burning inside of me. And it flared up the moment you walked in." She moved her hand to his semi-erect penis and stroked him.

"Are you going to be ready again?" she asked.

"You keep doing that and I am." He let his hand move from her thigh, down between her legs, where he found her wet.

"Oh yes," she gasped, "I'm ready when you are, Mr. Adams. But let's go slow, this time."

He rolled onto her, let his cock glide into her, and then took her slowly . . .

***

As he dressed, she said, "I thought you'd stay til morning, and then we'd go to the shop together."

"I'm hoping you'll give me that key. I can be there early, and when he leaves get right in. Then when you get there, we can go have breakfast."

She rolled over to the night table by the bed, opened a drawer and took out a key.

"Here you go," she said.

He accepted the key, put it in his pocket.

She laughed.

"Did you think I lied about the key just to get you here?" she asked.

"The thought had crossed my mind."

"Well, you'll find out for sure when you put the key into the lock, won't you?"

He went to the bed, kissed her and said, "I'll trust you."

He made his way through the dark house and out the front door. This had not been something he expected to happen that day but had actually gone better than he could have hoped for. The Candle Lady was a revelation in bed, and she had come up with the key to Culpepper's home. Clint only hoped that when he searched, something useful would turn up.

He walked back along her street to a larger one where he might be able to find a horse drawn cab to take him to his hotel. He wasn't going to get much sleep, though. With bank hours being what they were,

Culpepper would probably leave home at seven a.m., and Clint wanted to be there when he did.

Chapter Twenty-Seven

Bleary-eyed from lack of sleep, Clint stood across the street and watched Culpepper leave at seven-ten the next morning. He waited until the man was out of sight, then crossed the street and tried the key Amy had given him. As she had promised, it unlocked the door.

He took the stairs to the second floor and came to another door. He only had one key. He hoped it fit both doors. It did. He entered and closed the door behind him.

There were three rooms, if you called the small kitchen a room. There was a sitting room, a bedroom, and the kitchen. If Culpepper was stealing money from other depositors as well as Clint, he wasn't spending it here.

That thought had only just occurred to him. What if he wasn't the only one. The bank had connections to banks in other cities around the country. If they were careful to steal from out-of-towners, they might get away with it until somebody actually showed up—like Clint. That was something to talk to the bank manager Packer, about. Unless he was in on it. And what if Ingram, the president of the Denver bank, was in on it, too? And now he was dead.

Before leaving the hotel that morning, Clint had asked where the nearest telegraph office was. He'd forgotten to send the lieutenant in Denver a message, telling him where he was staying, as he had promised to do, so he got it done early.

The rooms were neat and clean. He started in the sitting room, looking everywhere, including underneath the cushions of the divan in the center of the room. When he came up empty he moved to the bedroom. He couldn't have said what he was looking for, just *something*.

He looked in all the drawers, underneath the mattress and the bed, behind the curtains, careful the whole time not to make a mess. Nothing.

That left the small kitchen.

There weren't many places to search there, but as he was turning to leave, he felt something beneath his foot. A closer look revealed a loose board. Of course, that's where lots of people hid things. He got down on his knees pried the board up, and then the one next to it. There was a metal box underneath. He took it out and opened it.

It was full of money.

He took the bills out and counted them. There was more than had been stolen from his account. He thought about taking his but decided against it. What if this was simply the man's life savings, and he had nothing to do with the theft? He couldn't be sure Culpepper was involved. He left the money where it was and replaced the boards. If and when he determined the man's guilt, he knew where to find the money. And if he was, indeed, guilty, he didn't want to tip him off. He also wanted the man who had walked into the bank, pretending to be him.

Finished with his search, he left the place, making sure to lock both the upstairs and downstairs doors behind him. He checked Amy's store and found the front door open. When he entered, she smiled from behind the counter.

"Did the key work?"

"Yes," he said, "on both doors."

"I'm relieved," she said.

"You didn't know if it would?"

She shrugged and said, "I never tried it. Time for breakfast?"

"Yes."

"Did you find anything?"

"Yes, and no," he said.

"What's that mean?"

"I'll tell you over breakfast," he said. "Where are we going?"

"Not far," she said. "A little place I know that does the best flapjacks."

"Sounds good. Lead the way."

Chapter Twenty-Eight

The place did, indeed, have great flapjacks, with bacon in them. Over two stacks he told Amy about his search.

"So you found your money," she said. "That's wonderful."

"I found money," he said. "I don't know if any of it is mine."

"Why don't you just take what's yours, leave the rest, and get out of town?" she asked.

"Because that would be stealing," he said. "I'm not only not a gunman, I'm not a thief, either."

"I'm sorry," she said, "I didn't mean—"

"It's all right."

"You're an honorable man," she said. "I'll bet you don't run into many of those. I know I don't."

"Not every day," he said, "but I have met a few."

"So what are you going to do now?"

"Talk to the bank manager again," he said, "and follow Culpepper some more. If he's in league with somebody, they'll have to meet up sooner or later. And I want both of them."

"And if he's innocent?"

"Then I'm back where I started, and out a lot of money," he said.

"Does that mean I'm buying breakfast?" she asked, with a smile.

***

Clint paid for breakfast and walked Amy back to her store.

"Will I see you again?"

Handing her back the key he said, "I'd bet on it."

She smiled, looked around, saw nobody on the street at that time of the morning, and kissed him. Then she went into her store.

Clint turned and made the walk back to the bank. As he entered, Culpepper spotted him from behind his cage and looked away. Clint decided to leave him alone, and instead went over to the desk where the girl, Angela, sat.

"Good-morning," he said.

She looked up at him and said, "Oh, good-morning. Can I help you, Mr. Adams?"

"Yes, I'd like to see Mr. Packer, again, if he's available," Clint said.

"I'm sure he is, but I'll check."

She went to Packer's office, came back with a smile.

"He'll see you," she said. "Go right in."

"Thank you."

Clint went to the manager's door and entered the office.

"Mr. Adams," Packer said, from behind his desk. "I'm afraid I have no news for you."

"That's okay," Clint said. "I just have a few questions about your man, Culpepper."

"Yes, well," Packer said, "he's usually very good at his job—"

"I understand that," Clint said. "I'm wondering what you think of the possibility that he may be involved with the theft."

Packer looked surprised.

"Oh, well," he said, "as shocked as I am that he made a mistake, I'd be even more shocked if he had done it on purpose—and expected to get away with it."

"I'm wondering if maybe I'm not the only victim," Clint said. "Have you had any other complaints?"

"Of this kind?" he asked. "Certainly not, or I'd know about it. Why would you think that?"

Clint didn't want to tell Packer about the money he found under Culpepper's floor.

"I was just thinking," he said, instead, "what if I'm the only one who traveled here to complain, and they've been getting away with it up to now?"

"They?"

"Yes, Culpepper and whoever he's working with."

"Look, I might fire him for mishandling your account, but for stealing? I just can't see it."

"Does he have any friends here at the bank?"

"No, he's a quiet man who keeps to himself."

"So nobody can tell me anything about him," Clint said.

"I just told you," Packer said. "He's quiet."

"Mr. Packer," Clint said, "I'm going to keep looking into this."

"As will I, sir," Packer said. "If I can get you your money back, I will."

After that statement Clint didn't want to accuse the man of also being part of the plot.

"All right, then," Clint said. "I'll continue to wait to hear from you at my hotel."

"I believe I'll have something to tell you in a day or two."

"I hope so," Clint said. "Thank you for seeing me."

"Of course."

Clint looked Culpepper's way as he left, but the teller kept his eyes averted.

Chapter Twenty-Nine

When Clint returned to his hotel, there was a message, but from Lieutenant Norman in Denver. It was short. NO PROGRESS. HOW ABOUT YOU? Clint decided to walk to the telegraph office and send a reply.

He sent: LITTLE PROGRESS, NOTHING DEFINITE. I'LL STAY IN TOUCH.

He left the telegraph office and headed back to the hotel. On the way he became aware of somebody following him. He stopped in front of a store, and the man ducked into a doorway. Clint had never seen him before.

He could have ducked into a store, waited for the man to get closer, then grab him and find out why he was following him. But he decided instead to lose him, then turn around and follow him.

This was interesting. Who would have sent someone to follow him? Only somebody from the bank, either Culpepper or Packer.

He started walking again, looking for an alley. Because he didn't know the streets, he decided to go all the way back to his hotel and use that building to lose the tail, and then turn the tables.

He entered the lobby of the hotel and stopped at the front desk.

"Is there a back way out of here?" he asked.

"Why?"

"There's somebody I'm trying to avoid."

"A husband?" The man smirked.

"You got it right the first time."

"Doorway behind me leads to a hall. At the end of the hall is the back door."

"Thanks." Clint moved behind the desk. "If he comes in . . ."

"I never saw you," the clerk said.

Clint handed him a few bills.

"Thanks."

Clint went down the hall and out the back door. Then he found the alley next to the hotel and took it to the street. He peered out and waited. Before long, the man who followed him came out of the hotel, looking puzzled. He looked up and down the street, then started walking.

He was tall, thin, in his thirties, wearing work clothes. He didn't look armed, but Clint was willing to bet he had a gun under his clothes somewhere.

Clint stepped out into the street and started to follow him.

***

It was a twenty-minute walk, but the man finally ducked into a saloon. He never looked behind him, had no idea anyone was following him.

Clint stopped in front and looked in the window. He expected to see the man meeting someone. Instead, he saw him buy a beer and sit at a table alone. Maybe he was waiting for someone.

Clint could have crossed the street and stepped into a doorway to watch the front of the saloon. If he did that, he'd have to run back across every time a man entered, to see if they were meeting. He couldn't do that. It would be too time consuming. He decided to simply go into the saloon, order a beer, and see what happened.

He walked in and approached the bar. It was early, so there weren't many customers. The man he had followed was staring into his beer, so he didn't see Clint enter. Clint wondered how long he could stand there and go unnoticed.

"Help ya?" the big bartender asked. He was mean looking, in his thirties, with broad shoulders, and bulging arms.

"Beer."

He drew the beer and put it on the bar. The glass was dirty. Clint didn't touch it.

"The man at the table over my right shoulder," Clint said. "Who is he?"

The bartender looked at the man, then back at Clint. "Don't know."

"Yeah, you do," Clint said.

"Why do you wanna know?"

"I think I might know him."

"No you don't."

"No," Clint said, "I don't. But I may have to kill him."

The man firmed his jaw.

"Not in here."

"If I have to kill him," Clint said, "I may have to kill you, too."

"Now, wait a minute." Suddenly he looked less mean, and more apprehensive.

"What's his name?"

"Casey . . . something. I dunno. He comes in here a lot, but we ain't friends."

"Does he meet anyone else in here?"

"Not usually," the bartender said. "This ain't exactly a friendly place."

"I got that feeling," Clint said. "You got a shotgun under the bar?"

The man swallowed.

"Yeah."

"Leave it there," Clint said. "If you bring it out, I *will* kill you. Got it?"

"I understand."

Clint pushed the beer away.

"I don't want that," he said. "Dump it out and wash that glass."

He turned and walked to the table where the man was sitting.

Chapter Thirty

"Casey?"

The man looked up and his eyes widened. He looked around, as if seeking help, and his hand went inside his shirt.

"You know who I am?" Clint asked.

Casey swallowed and nodded.

"If you bring out a gun, it'll be the last thing you ever do. You believe me?"

Sweating, Casey nodded.

"Wait," Clint said, sitting across from him, "I have a better idea. Take the gun out, slowly, and push it across the table to me."

Casey swallowed, took a derringer out from inside his shirt. He put it on the table and pushed it across. Clint took it and tucked it into his belt.

"Good, now we can talk."

"Um, about w-what?" Casey asked.

"About why you were following me."

"I wasn't—"

"Don't lie to me, Casey," Clint said. "Why were you following me?"

"I dunno."

"You don't know?"

"It was j-just a job," Casey said.

"What was the job?" Clint asked. "Follow me and do what?"

"J—just watch, see what you do, where you go," Casey said. "Look, Mister, I just do odd jobs."

"For who?"

"Anybody who'll pay me."

"Okay, Casey," Clint said, "this part is important. Who paid you to follow me?"

"Just a guy."

"How did he find you?"

"I spend time in a few places," Casey said. "He left word in one of them that he needed a job done."

"Is this one of the places?"

"Naw, I just come here once in a while for a beer," Casey said. "I don't get messages here."

"Casey," Clint said, "I'm not about to believe that you took a job from somebody whose name you don't know."

"Aw, come on, Mister," Casey said. "If I give you a name, people ain't gonna hire me no more."

"What did you think when he told you who you were following?" Clint asked.

Casey licked his lips.

"I—I raised my price."

"And he paid it?"

"Half," Casey said. "I'm supposed to collect the other half."

"Directly from him?"

"He said either him or his partner."

"Do you know his partner's name?"

"No."

"But you know his name, don't you?"

Casey nodded.

"Okay, Casey," Clint said. "Tell me his name and this will all be over."

Casey shifted his feet, nervously. Clint could smell his fear.

"Y-you ain't gonna kill me?"

"Not today," Clint said.

Casey licked his dry lips, drank some of his beer to lubricate his mouth. Clint was prepared for him to try and throw the rest of it in his face, maybe make a break for it, but it didn't happen.

"Casey?"

"His name is Brannigan," Casey stammered, "C-Cash Brannigan."

"And where can I find Mr. Brannigan?"

"He's usually at a saloon called The Lion's Den. It's on Palmer Street."

"That's it, Casey," Clint said, standing.

Casey looked relieved.

"Oh, one more thing," Clint said.

"W-what?"

"What's your last name?"

"Fuller, I'm Casey Fuller."

"If any of this is a lie, Casey Fuller," Clint said. "I'll find you. You believe me?"

"Yessir."

"Don't follow me again."

"No, sir."

"If you do—"

"I got it, sir," Casey said. "Believe me, I understand. Never again."

"Good."

Clint turned, looked at the bartender, exchanged a nod and left.

Casey almost fainted, but he mustered up the strength to walk to the bar.

"One more beer, and a whiskey."

Chapter Thirty-One

After Clint left the little saloon and Casey Fuller, he went to his hotel.

"Everything okay?" the clerk asked, as he walked by.

"Worked out just fine," Clint said. "Thanks."

He went to his room and sat on the bed. He had to admit he had expected Casey to tell him that a man named Culpepper, or Packer, had hired him. Brannigan was a new name, but maybe that was the man who actually went into the bank and pretended to be him, in order to withdraw the money.

So now he had to go and find this man Cash Brannigan and face him down, find out who he was, what he did, and what he wanted.

***

Cash Brannigan waited at the Lion's Den, but Casey Fuller never showed up. Either he was still following Clint Adams, or Adams had spotted him and killed him. Brannigan finished his beer and stood up. There was no longer any point in waiting for that idiot, Fuller. He never should have hired him in the first place. If it turned out that the Gunsmith wanted a face-to-face, Brannigan would give it to him.

" 'nother one, Cash?" the bartender asked.

"Later, Billy," Brannigan said. "I've got things to do."

Brannigan went out the front door.

***

Fifteen minutes after Cash Brannigan left, Clint Adams walked in. The Lion's Den was a small saloon, but it was neat and clean, which was a switch from what he had seen, so far.

He went to the bar. The bartender had been at the other end, talking to two men. When he saw Clint, he came over.

"Can I help you?"

"I'm looking for a man named Cash Brannigan," Clint said. "I'm told he spends time here."

"Cash?" the bartender said, with a laugh. "That's a name?"

"That's the name I got," Clint said.

The bartender yelled down to the two men he had been talking to.

"You fellas ever hear of a fella named Cash?"

"Cash?" one of them said, with a laugh. "That's a name?"

"That's what this fella says."

Clint looked at the bartender, then at the other two men. He was convinced they were all lying. That meant he was going to have to do more than just ask about Brannigan.

"Thanks for your help," Clint said.

"You want a beer, while you're here?" the barman asked.

"Sure, why not?" Clint said.

The bartender served him, then leaned on the bar.

"So what kind of fella is this Cash?" he asked.

"I can't tell you," Clint said. "I never met him."

"Then why you looking for him?"

Clint decided to almost tell the truth.

"He owes money."

"Ah," the bartender said. "A man named Cash owes you money. That's funny."

"You know what?" Clint said. "You're right, that is funny." He sipped the beer, left most of it. "Thanks for the drink." He dropped two bits on the bar and turned to leave the saloon but stopped.

"I don't suppose you've heard of a man called Culpepper?" he said.

"Nope," the man said, "but that's another funny name, ain't it?"

"I guess it is," Clint said, and left.

***

The bartender waited a few minutes to give Clint time to walk away, then looked down at the two men.

"One of you better go find Cash," he said. "Tell him the Gunsmith was here, looking for him."

"That was the Gunsmith?" one of the men asked.

"That's what I figure," the bartender said. "Cash said he was mixed up in something involving the Gunsmith. Seems like it's money."

"Why would he get mixed up with the Gunsmith?" the second man asked.

"Why does Cash do anything?" the bartender said.

The first man said, "I'll go and find 'im."

"I'll come with ya," the second man offered.

They both left the saloon, which left the bartender there alone.

***

Clint decided to wait down the street in a doorway and see what happened. Sure enough, the two men from the end of the bar came out. He gave them a head start, then stepped from the doorway and followed.

Chapter Thirty-Two

Clint followed the two men for half the day, but they seemed to be doing the same thing he was doing, looking for Cash Brannigan. They went into several saloons and restaurants, then came out and kept going. Clint was getting tired of trailing behind, so he decided to change tactics. He headed for the bank, again.

He got himself situated outside before the bank closed. Within half an hour Culpepper came out and started his walk home. Clint decided to follow him openly, this time, and see what that brought.

He dropped in right behind Culpepper, who walked several blocks before he finally turned around and faced Clint.

"W-what are you doing?" he asked.

"Following you."

"Follow—why?"

"I want to see where you go."

"I'm going home," the teller said. "Where did you think I was going?"

"I don't know," Clint said. "Maybe to meet Cash Brannigan?"

"Cash—is that a name?"

"It is," Clint said. "He was your accomplice when you stole my money."

"That's what this is about?" Culpepper said. "Mr. Adams, I made a mistake—"

"You sure did."

Suddenly, instead of seeming nervous, Culpepper became angry.

"You can't do this!" he snapped. "I didn't do anything!"

"That's what I'm trying to find out, Culpepper," Clint said, "Just what you did."

"If you keep following me, I'll go to the law."

He could have told Culpepper about the money under the floorboards, but he decided to keep that in his pocket for later.

"Go right ahead," Clint said. "I'd like to talk to the law."

"Look," Culpepper said, pointing his finger at Clint, "I'm going home. If you want to follow me, be my guest."

"Well, thanks for your permission," Clint said, "but I was going to do that anyway."

Culpepper just shook his head in disgust, turned and started walking.

Clint fell in behind him.

***

From across the street Cash Brannigan watched Culpepper turn and face the Gunsmith. The teller had guts, he had to give him that. Brains and guts, since emptying the bank accounts was his idea.

Brannigan figured he would only need one shot from there to kill the Gunsmith, but that would have attracted a lot of attention on the street, and it would have brought the law into things. Since Adams was obviously following Culpepper home, Brannigan decided to just let them be. He was going to have to figure a way to get to Culpepper without the Gunsmith seeing him. He watched the two of them walk away, waited until they were out of sight, then stepped out into the open and walked the other way.

***

Clint watched Culpepper put his key in his door, unlock it and go inside. He could have gone into the candle shop to see Amy, but he wasn't ready for that, yet. He wanted to get back to the bank and see if he could catch Packer leaving.

Hell, he had been following so any people lately, why not follow the bank manager, as well? It would certainly be easier to empty bank accounts with the manager's help.

He got to the bank and took up a position across the street. He saw the girl, Angela, leave, and then Packer stepped out and locked the door. The manager started walking up the street, in the opposite direction Culpepper had gone. Clint gave him a bit of a head start, and then stepped out and followed.

***

Packer went to dinner.

He stopped in an expensive looking restaurant that was about five blocks from the bank. Clint was hungry and didn't want to wait across the street while Packer had himself a good meal. He decided to join the man.

He entered the restaurant, and when a man in a black suit asked if he could help him, Clint said, "I'm meeting someone, and there he is."

"Of course, sir," the host said. "Follow me."

When they reached the manager's table, he looked up at them in surprise.

"Mr. Packer," the host said, "your guest has arrived."

"Thank you," Clint said. He pulled out the chair across from Packer and sat. The manager was still staring. "What's good here?" Clint asked.

Chapter Thirty-Three

Packer gathered himself in.

"Mr. Adams," he said. "What a coincidence seeing you here."

"I was passing by and this place looked good," Clint said. "Then when I came in and saw you sitting here, I decided to join you. I hope you don't mind."

"No, no, not at all," Packer said. "As far as what's good, I have to say. . . everything. They have a wonderful chef, here."

"Then I might as well just have a steak," Clint said, "and see what he does with that."

"Ah," Packer said, "when he cooks a steak, he finishes it off with butter, and then some bourbon."

"Sounds good."

When the waiter came over, Packer let Clint order his steak first, and a beer, then said, "I'll have the Veal Piccata, Henry."

"Of course, sir."

"It's an Italian dish," Packer told Clint.

"I figured that out," Clint said.

"Oh, I'm sorry," Packer said, "I didn't mean . . . it's very good."

The waiter brought Packer a glass of white wine, and Clint a mug of beer, along with a basket of biscuits, and butter.

"I'm sorry, but I don't have any information for you, yet," Packer said.

"That's okay," Clint said. "I have some for you."

"Really?"

"Yes," Clint said, "Your man Culpepper is working with someone named Cash Brannigan."

"Cash?" Packer said. "Is that a name?"

"It is."

"Who is he?"

"I believe he's the man who came into your bank, pretending to be me."

"So you're telling me that Culpepper definitely took part in this theft?"

"Indeed," Clint said, "that's what I'm telling you."

"My God!" Packer said. "I'm shocked. I suppose I had better call the police."

"No, not yet," Clint said. "Give me a chance to get my money back from them before you do that."

"Can you do that?"

"I believe I can," Clint said. "I want to reclaim my money and find this man Brannigan. Then we can give both of them to the law."

"Well," Packer said, "it's your money."

"And your bank," Clint said. "You still need to determine if they've done this to other accounts."

"I'll need to bring in the bank accountants for that," Packer said.

"So we both have work to do, then," Clint said, "but we can do it after this fine meal, eh?"

"Indeed," Packer said.

***

When the meals came, Clint saw what Packer had meant. The steak was cooked perfectly, red in the center, and it had a flavor he had never experienced before. He didn't know if it was from the butter, the bourbon, or both.

Packer gave all his attention to his thinly sliced veal, so Clint did the same, and they both ate in relative silence, except for a comment or two.

When both their plates were clean Packer asked, "So what did you think?"

"It was delicious," Clint said. "You weren't lying about the chef."

"Dessert, gents?" the waiter asked.

"Not for me," Clint said. "I have to be going. Can I get my bill?"

"Nonsense," Packer said. "The dinner is on me. You're doing a service for the bank by exposing these thefts."

"If there are more," Clint said.

"That's what the accountants will find out," Packer said. "I'll contact them in the morning."

"Good," Clint said. "I'll see you soon, Mr. Packer."

As Clint walked away, he heard Packer ordering pie and coffee.

***

After Clint left, he thought about waiting outside and following Packer again, but he decided against it. Instead, he walked back to Amy's candle shop. But as he approached, he saw her come out the door that led to Culpepper's place. He ducked into a doorway as she stopped and looked up and down the street, then went into her store.

What was she doing up there? He now realized how quickly she had decided to seduce him, and he had let her. Now he was wondering if she was involved.

Suddenly he suspected everybody.

Chapter Thirty-Four

Clint sat on the bed in his room, holding the Schofield in his hand. He had the feeling everyone was lying to him: Packer, Culpepper, Amy. And he needed to find Cash Brannigan. He wondered which of the four of them was the brains behind their activities. The only way to find that out was probably to use his gun.

Judging from his meetings with them, he tried to guess which one would scare the most. Amy because she was a woman? Packer? Culpepper? Maybe it was Brannigan who was pulling their strings. He needed one of them to tell him.

On the way back to his hotel he had stopped in the telegraph office again. He sent Lt. Norman a telegram that said: I HAVE FOUR NAMES. He gave Norman the names and asked if he recognized any of them? Then he asked the policeman to find out what he could about each person. He expected to get a reply the next day. That gave him the rest of the night to think things over, or to do something.

He could go to the candle shop, go home with Amy, and when they were in her bedroom, make her talk. Or he could go to Culpepper's home, stick his gun in his face and take the money from underneath the floorboards. His money, and whatever else was there. Then they would have to do something to get it all back.

Or he could go back to the Lion's Den and use his gun to get some answers about Cash Brannigan. Because they had all lied to him when he was there.

He stood up and holstered his gun, then picked up his hat and left the room.

***

When he entered the Lion's Den again, it was as if no one had moved since the last time he was there. The same bartender was behind the bar, and the same two men standing at the end. Clint remained standing just inside the door.

"I want Cash Brannigan," he answered.

"I told you," the bartender said, "I don't know—"

"You're lying, and so are they," Clint said. "Now, somebody's going to talk right now, or somebody's going to die. Which will it be?"

The two men stood up straight. They both had guns in holsters on their hips.

The bartender had a shotgun beneath the bar. Clint wondered which of these men were going to call the play here. Then he decided none of them would. He drew his gun and fired twice. Both men looked down and saw that their guns and holsters were gone. They had been shot off their hips and were on the floor somewhere behind them.

"Now, wait—" one of them said.

Clint looked at the bartender. He had one hand on top of the bar, and one underneath. He was either going to produce the shotgun, or he was going to fire it right through the flimsy front of the bar.

"Make up your mind," Clint said, "but if you miss, you're dead."

The bartender firmed his jaw. Sweat trickled down from his forehead. Then he brought his hand out from under the bar empty and put both hands in the air.

"You fellas all know Cash Brannigan," Clint said.

"Uh, y-yeah, w-we do," the bartender said.

Clint looked at the two men, who were still shaking from his display of marksmanship.

"Then one of you is going to tell him that I want to see him," Clint said.

"We can't—" one of the men started.

"Yeah, you can," Clint said. "Deliver my message. And if he makes me search for him, he won't be happy when I find him."

"A-are you gonna kill 'im?" the barman asked.

"That's not the plan," Clint said, "but in the end, that'll be up to him."

"W-what do we tell 'im you want?" one of the men asked.

"To talk," Clint said, "just to talk."

"Where?" the bartender asked.

"Tell him I'm at the Rialto Hotel," Clint said. "I'll wait there for him tomorrow. Tell him I know his whole operation and want to talk to him about it."

"W-what operation?" one of the men asked.

"We don't know anythin' about an operation."

"No," Clint said, "you don't. I believe you. But he'll know what I'm talking about."

The three men looked at each other.

"I don't care which of you delivers my message but see that he gets it."

"Yeah, okay," the bartender said.

"After I leave," Clint said, "you can go and do what you want. But if you come out this door with guns in your hand—"

"We won't," the bartender said.

"No," one of the other men said, "we won't."

"Good." Clint holstered his gun and backed out of the saloon.

Chapter Thirty-Five

Clint found himself almost wishing somebody would shoot at him. At least if that happened, he would know how to handle it. Dealing with banking problems was a little outside his experience. Sticking his gun in somebody's face would probably get something done. He just had to decide whose face it would be. Packer's? Culpepper's? Brannigan's? And what about Amy Locane? Why would she be coming out of Culpepper's door when she said they didn't talk much?

Clint went over his dinner with Packer and decided if the bank manager was bringing in accountants to look at the records, then he probably wasn't involved. And just because Amy had gone upstairs to see Culpepper didn't mean she was involved, either.

The money underneath Culpepper's floorboards put him squarely in the frame, as far as Clint was concerned. And since he didn't think the man could have done it alone, that put Brannigan in there, with him.

Brannigan and Culpepper.

When he got back to his hotel, the clerk waved some papers at him from the desk.

"Thank you."

He took the messages to his room before reading them. One was a telegram from Lt. Norman in Denver. It was brief. Norman had no information on any of the names.

The other wasn't a telegram just a message. He thought it might be from the banker, but it was from Brannigan.

It said: MEET ME AT THE DEL RIO SALOON AT SEVEN O'CLOCK TOMORROW NIGHT. Now all Clint had to do was find the Del Rio Saloon.

***

After an uneventful next day, Clint asked the desk clerk if he knew of a saloon called The Del Rio. The man said yes, it was a long walk, or a short cab ride. Clint opted for the cab.

He got to the Del Rio at six-forty-five. Since he had no idea what Brannigan looked like, he simply got a beer from the bar and carried it to a back table. The place was empty, except for the bartender and another man standing at the bar. He decided rather than asking about Cash Brannigan, he was just going to wait.

He thought the man at the bar might be him, but that man was tall and lean, in his thirties, and didn't pay any attention to him. Also, that man was not wearing a gun.

At seven-oh-five a tall, beefy man in his forties, with a holstered pistol on his right hip, entered the saloon. Instinctively, Clint knew this was Brannigan. The man did not look around, simply went to the bar, ordered a beer, then carried it to the table.

"Clint Adams?" he asked, in a deep bass.

"That's right. Are you Cash Brannigan?"

"I am. Whataya want?"

"I want my money."

"What makes you think I got your money?"

"You don't have it," Clint said. "Your partner does. I know that."

"And who's my partner?" he asked.

"Culpepper," Clint said. "He's got the money under his floorboards."

Brannigan stared at Clint, who figured he had just surprised the man.

"I don't know what the hell you're talkin' about," Brannigan said.

"If you didn't," Clint said, "you wouldn't be here, right now."

"So you're just expectin' me to confess?"

"Mr. Brannigan," Clint said, "I don't care if you confess or not, I've got you and your partner figured. Now I'm just going to get my money back from both of you."

"And how are you gonna do that?" Brannigan asked. "With your gun?"

"If I have to," Clint said.

"Sacramento is a big city, Adams," Brannigan said, "not the Wild West."

"You're wearing a gun, Brannigan," Clint said. "When you wear a gun, you have to be prepared to use it."

"And I am, if it comes to that," Brannigan said. "You can count on it."

"And what would make it come to that? Asking for money back?"

"If I knew about your money—"

"I'll get it out of Culpepper, then," Clint said. "And if you want to try and stop me, go ahead."

"I think we're done, here," Brannigan said.

"We might be done *here*," Clint said, "but I've got to tell you, we're far from done."

Brannigan stood up.

"I'm going after Culpepper for my money next," Clint said. You want to see who gets there first?"

Clint watched Brannigan leave, then stood up and followed him out the door.

Chapter Thirty-Six

Clint headed for the Candle Lady, wondering if Culpepper would be home? Or would he be out meeting Brannigan somewhere? Hopefully, that money was still under the floorboards.

He stopped in front of the building. There was a light in the candle shop, which was supposed to be closed. Should he stop in and see Amy first, or just go upstairs? He decided to go into the shop, if only to get the key from Amy again.

As he entered the shop, Amy looked up from something she was wrapping.

"Well, hello," she said. "What brings you here?"

"I could ask you the same thing," he said. "Isn't it after closing?"

"I guess I lost track of time," she said. "I had some work to catch up on."

"Have you heard any movement upstairs?"

"From Culpepper's? No."

"Anybody come around, trying to get up there?"

"No."

"Do you have his key here?"

"Yes," she said. "Do you want it?"

"Please."

She opened a drawer, took out the key and handed it to him.

"Be careful," she said.

"I'll be right back."

Clint went outside, used the key on the downstairs door, went up the stairs and knocked on the door.

"Culpepper? You in there?" he called out.

When there was no answer, he knocked again. When there was still no answer, he used the key and opened the door. He saw Culpepper right away, lying on the floor. He hurried over to him, but there was a lot of blood, and the man was deathly pale. He crouched over him and saw the stab wounds on his chest and neck. He was definitely dead.

"No," he said, "no, no, no . . ."

He stood up, hurried over to where the loose floorboards were. They had been pried up, and the money was gone.

"Damn it!" he snapped.

He had lost his money, again.

***

Clint hurried back down the stairs to the candle shop, because something occurred to him. Why was the shop open so late, and what was Amy wrapping when he walked in? And why had he seen her coming out of Culpepper's that time?

When he got to the shop door it was closed and locked.

Brannigan had not seemed like the knife type, not the way he wore his gun. If he had killed Culpepper and taken the money, he would have shot him.

He pressed his face to the window and peered inside. Nobody was inside. Why had Amy locked up and left when he told her he would be right back down? What if the package she was wrapping was not candles, but the money?

Clint, not knowing where Brannigan was, hurried to Amy's house. If she was involved, then she was working with Brannigan. Maybe they were both there, getting ready to run off with the proceeds of their thefts.

When he reached the house, he knocked on the door, fully expecting there would be no answer. So he was surprised when she opened the door.

"There you are," he said. "I wondered where you went. I told you I'd be right back."

"I'm so sorry," she said, "I misunderstood. I thought you were going to come here. What happened with Mr. Culpepper? Was he there?"

"He's there, all right," Clint said. "He's dead."

"What?"

"He's dead, stabbed, and the money's gone," Clint said, entering the house. "Are you sure you didn't hear a sound from upstairs?"

"Well . . ."

"What is it?"

"I did hear a thud, but I just thought he—he dropped something."

"More like somebody dropped him."

She covered her mouth with her hands.

"You mean . . . somebody murdered him upstairs while I was downstairs?"

"That's what it looks like," he said.

That shook her.

"What will you do now?"

"I think I better contact the police," Clint said. "As far as Culpepper's murder goes, let them solve it. I just want my money back."

"But how will you get it now?"

He thought a moment before answering.

"There's still one way," he said.

"And what's that?"

"I'll tell you later," he said. "After I go for the police."

Chapter Thirty-Seven

Clint waved down a cab and told the driver to take him to the nearest Police Station. When the man dropped him off, he went inside and said, he wanted to report a murder. The policeman at the desk frowned at him, then said, "I think maybe you better show us."

***

Clint went with two uniformed Sacramento policemen to the scene of the murder. He still had the key, so he let them in and went upstairs with them.

"There he is," Clint said, pointing.

"Somebody was mad at this guy," one of them said. "Look at those stab wounds."

"We're gonna need an ambulance, and that detective they hired," the older man said. "Wait here with him."

"But wait—"

"I won't be long," the older policeman said. "I'll get somebody to run me over to the station."

"Okay," the younger one said.

The older man went down the stairs.

"This man worked at the bank—" Clint started to explain.

"Save it," the policeman said. "There's gonna be somebody here real soon to get your story."

The person who came to get his story was an older man who said his name was Detective Stites.

"Let's go downstairs," he said to Clint, "so we don't get interrupted."

As they started to leave, the two uniformed policemen put their heads together and laughed.

"What was that about?" Clint asked, as he and the detective got downstairs.

"They think it's funny that I left New York to come here," Stites said.

"Why'd you leave New York?" Clint asked.

"I was told the weather would be good for me," Stites answered. "You wanna tell me how you came to find this body?"

Clint told Stites the whole story, going back to Denver and Lieutenant Norman.

"I'll contact Norman and see how he's doing with his murder," Stites said. "Maybe they're connected." He closed his notebook. "I'll go up and look the scene over."

"Do you want me to come up with you?"

"That's not necessary. Like I said, I'll contact Norman, I'll talk to Packer at the bank. What hotel are you at?"

"The Rialto."

"Then I know where to find you," Stites said. "You can leave."

As Stites turned to go back upstairs, Clint wondered if he should tell him about Amy Locane and Cash Brannigan? Then he thought, no, they were still his best chance to get his money back. He didn't want it to end up the evidence in a murder, because then it would be a long time before he saw it again.

"Okay, then," Clint said, "I'll be on my way, but . . . won't those two funny men upstairs wonder how you could let me leave?"

"Mr. Adams, you're the Gunsmith," Stites said, "I know your reputation. I never heard nothin' about you usin' a knife. If you killed this guy, he'd be shot. You can go."

Clint decided not to argue any further. Stites went upstairs, and Clint walked away.

***

So now the question was, who had his money, Brannigan or Amy? And which of them had killed Culpepper?

Stites' logic as to why Clint wasn't the killer also worked for Brannigan. If he had killed Culpepper, the teller probably would've been shot. But was Amy Locane, the Candle Lady, a thief and a murderess?

Amy was the most available one to Clint. At least he knew where she was—if she was still in her house. She could have lit out with the money after he left her. And if she had killed Culpepper, that would make sense. The only way to find out was to go back there.

When he arrived at her house, he paused a moment before approaching it. He watched from across the street, wondering if Brannigan might show up there. If he saw the police at Culpepper's and found out the teller was dead, he might have come here looking for Amy, also. But Clint gave it enough time, and Brannigan neither appeared at the house, nor came out of the house. Clint could see activity through the window, which looked like Amy was home—and alive.

Finally, he left his doorway across the street and approached the front door. He knocked, and almost immediately Amy opened the door.

"Oh, thank God!" she said, when she saw him. "I was worried about you."

"Oh? Why's that?" Clint asked.

"I thought maybe you'd been arrested for killing Mr. Culpepper," she said. "I mean, what with your reputation, and all."

"Actually," Clint said, "it was my reputation that convinced them to let me go."

"Well, come in" she said, "you can tell me about it over supper."

"You cooked?"

She closed the door and turned to face him.

"Well, I thought, if they didn't arrest you, you'd probably be hungry."

Was she cold and calculating enough to have killed Culpepper, and then come home to cook supper?

Chapter Thirty-Eight

While Clint enjoyed the food Amy had cooked, he couldn't help staring across the table at her, wondering if she was a cold-blooded killer?

"What do you intend to do now?"

"What I've been doing," he said. "Get my money back."

"Still?" she asked. "The murder of poor Mr. Culpepper does nothing to change your mind?"

"Just the opposite," Clint said. "Somebody killed him, probably to keep his mouth shut. I'm not going to let them get away with it."

"Are you going to kill whoever it is?" she asked.

"That was never my plan," Clint said. "They stole my money and I want it back. Now that they've killed Culpepper, it'll be up to the law to make them pay."

"Do you have any idea who killed Mr. Culpepper?" she asked.

"Let's say I have an inkling," Clint said.

"Can you tell me who you think it was?" she asked.

"No, not yet."

"Am I in danger, in my shop?" she asked. "Shouldn't I know who to be on the lookout for?"

"Not if what happened upstairs has nothing to do with you," he said, watching her carefully. There was no reaction.

After supper she asked him to stay, but he said he couldn't.

"I'm expecting something at my hotel," he said. "I have to get back there."

"Something that will help you?"

"I sure hope so," he said. "Why don't I stop in your shop tomorrow and tell you what's going on?"

"Please do," she said. "I'll just want to know that you're all right."

She walked him to the door, kissed him good-night and said, "Please be careful."

"I always am," he said, and left.

***

He didn't leave the area right away. He spent a few minutes across the street once again, just to see if she would be leaving her house. When she didn't, and it became very dark, he decided to simply return to his hotel.

As he entered the lobby, he wouldn't have been surprised to find Detective Stites there, but apparently the man still felt that the Gunsmith was not responsible for Culpepper's death.

He stopped at the desk to ask about telegrams or messages, but there were none.

"But," the clerk said, "there was a man here looking for you earlier."

"Did he leave his name?" Clint asked.

"No, but he was a rather large man, wearing a gun," the clerk said. "He actually looked quite mean."

Brannigan.

"Did he leave a message?"

"No, sir."

"Okay, thanks."

Clint went up to his room, opened the door very carefully, with his hand hovering near the Schofield, just in case Brannigan was inside.

The room was empty.

He turned up the lamp, hung his gunbelt on the bedpost, and sat on the bed. He thought about Cash Brannigan and Amy Locane. He wondered why he was thinking of them as separate entities? It was more than likely they were working together. If he could catch them together, he would be killing two birds with the same stone.

He decided to turn in and worry about the two of them the next morning. But just to be on the safe side, he jammed the back of a wooden chair underneath the doorknob before going to sleep.

***

In the morning he rose feeling an emptiness inside of him. Only it wasn't just hunger. He felt like he had lost a friend. He was now convinced that Amy Locane was involved somehow, with the theft, the murder, or both. She was now a lost friend to him.

He wanted to have an uninterrupted breakfast, so he decided to leave the hotel and find a new place to eat. Several blocks away he found a small café with the name on the window, but some of the letters had flaked off, so he really couldn't tell what it was called. Still, he went inside. He ordered ham-and-eggs simply because it was a pretty hard dish for anybody to ruin.

The interior was small. Although he sat against the back wall, he could still see out the window, through the flaking letters. Nobody knew he was there, though, so he could eat and think. But what was there to think about? The thinking was over. It was time to do something.

After breakfast.

Chapter Thirty-Nine

After breakfast he went to the bank. Angela took him in to see Packer.

"The accountants will be here later today," the manager said. "By this afternoon we should know something."

"I think I know something now," Clint said.

"Oh?"

"Yes," Clint said, "I've crossed your name off my list."

Packer looked surprised, then pleased.

"I suppose I should appreciate that."

"I just figured you'd never send for accountants if you had something to hide."

"You're probably right," Packer said. "I don't suppose you'd like a job as a teller? I happen to be short one."

"I don't think you're going to miss him very much," Clint said. "Detective Stites was here?"

"Oh yes, asking many questions," Packer said. "I wasn't going to tell him about the money, but it seems you already did."

"Yeah, sorry about that," Clint said. "I felt I had to tell him the truth."

"Well, he'll be back to find out what the accountants discover," Packer said.

"I think I already know what they'll find," Clint said, "but you can tell him. It might help him find his killer."

"Do you believe you're close to getting your money back?" Packer asked.

"I do."

"And if there are other accounts that have been emptied?" he asked. "Can you get that money back?"

"Possibly," Clint said. "It all depends on if the thieves been saving it or spending it."

"The bank would appreciate anything you could do," Packer said. "And I mean, with a reward."

Clint smiled.

"If I get a reward, I won't be depositing it in your bank."

"I understand that."

Clint stood up.

"I'll check back with you at the end of the day."

"I'll have something for you," Packer said. "I'll tell you before I tell Detective Stites."

"I appreciate that," Clint said, and left the office. He noticed on the way out that Angela wasn't at her desk but was behind Culpepper's teller's cage. She was probably filling in.

***

When he walked into the Lion's Den, the bartender was alone. When he saw Clint, he put his hands out in front of him.

"Not again," he said.

"Relax," Clint said. "Get me a beer."

The bartender did as he was told. He never let his hands go down below the level of the bar.

"Whataya want?" he asked.

Clint sipped his beer.

"I want to know where Cash Brannigan lives."

"How would I know that?" the barman asked.

"Because you're his friend," Clint said. "You and those other two. But they don't know where he lives. I'll bet you do."

"Didn't you and him talk?"

"We did," Clint said, "and I want to talk to him again."

"I can tell 'im —"

"No," Clint said, "this time I want to go to him and talk. Where does he live?"

"I can't—" the bartender started, then stopped. "He'll kill me if I do."

"I'll kill you if you don't," Clint said. "So the question is, do you want to die now, or later?"

***

The building looked like a warehouse. What would Brannigan be doing living there? Maybe the bartender had lied. But Clint thought he was too scared for that.

While he was standing there, several men came and went. It didn't seem as if anyone needed a key for the front door. It was early, and the street was empty. He crossed over, found the door unlocked, and entered the building.

The inside was dark and cavernous, with a high roof. On both sides, along the walls, were boxes of differing sizes. He wasn't curious about what was in them, so he kept moving, further into the building.

When he came to the end of that floor, he found a doorway that led to stairs. There was a second floor, but it wasn't directly above that cavernous room. It was in the back of the building.

He opened the door and went up the stairs. At the top he found another door. This one was locked. The door was too solid to force. He would need a key to get in.

Wearily, he went back down the stairs, realizing that he was going to have to, once again, keep watch. He wished he was on his Tobiano, riding an open trail.

Chapter Forty

Was the money that important?

What he had lost had been earned over a number of years, but it wasn't a fortune. The only way the thieves were making money was by looting multiple accounts. He could have left it to the bank accountants and the police to solve the problem. But if word got out that the Gunsmith had been robbed, and had done nothing about it, he would become a target.

So he couldn't let it go. He went back across the street and settled in to watch the building. There was more coming and going, but none of the men were Cash Brannigan. By late afternoon he thought his best bet might be Amy Locane. He had been hoping that if Brannigan hadn't killed Culpepper, he would implicate Amy. But if she admitted to her involvement, maybe she could point him to Brannigan.

Then something occurred to him. Without Culpepper they no longer had an in at the bank. Their looting of bank accounts was over. Whatever amount of money they now had was going to have to be enough—but was it enough for the two of them? Maybe he could convince

Amy that her life was in danger, and then she would talk.

Clint had to admit that, through all of this, he could have used Talbot Roper's help. As a detective Clint was at most a talented amateur, but Roper was the best, and probably could have wrapped this up by now. Clint had to make do without Roper, and without his modified Colt. The Schofield still felt odd on his hip, and in his hand.

He had told Amy he would be dropping by her shop today to fill her in, so he decided to do just that.

***

When he walked into the Candle Lady, a look of relief came over Amy's face. If she was an actress, she was a good one.

"Omigod, I've been so worried," she admitted.

"Why?"

"You said you'd drop by this morning," she said, "and now it's almost closing time. What've you been doing?"

"Trying to find a man named Cash Brannigan," he said.

"Cash?" she said. "Is that a name?"

"It is," he said. "He worked with Culpepper, a big, mean looking gent with a gun on his hip. You sure you never saw him come by here?"

"You're the meanest looking man with a gun I've seen come by here," she told him. "He was Mr. Culpepper's accomplice?"

"One of them," he said.

"There are more?"

"I believe one more," Clint said, "and I believe that he may have the money." She didn't seem to be aware that he was talking about her.

"So you're trying to find Brannigan so he can lead you to the other one?"

"I think they both might be thinking about killing the other and keeping all the money," Clint said. "I'm hoping to catch them before that can happen."

"And how close do you think you are?"

"I've had one conversation with Brannigan," Clint said, "and I believe he's also looking for me. We just have to get together, and I think we might get some answers."

"And that's why you have no time for me," she said.

"I'm sorry—"

"Don't apologize," she said. "You never expected me to come waltzing into your life. You need to do what you set out to do. I understand."

"Thanks for that," he said. "Have you talked with your landlord about upstairs?"

"Yes," she said, "he's not going to be looking to rent it out until the police find out who killed Mr. Culpepper."

"I guess that makes sense."

"Do you still think I'm safe here?" she asked. "Or should I be on the lookout for that mean looking Mr. Brannigan?"

"I don't see any reason why he'd bother you," he said. "You should be safe." Then, making it sound like a joke, he added, "Unless you're his accomplice."

"Me?" she asked. "You're joking."

"Yes," he lied, "I am."

***

As he left the Candle Lady, Amy told him she would be closing and going home. He felt he needed to trail her, and watch her go inside, just to be sure Brannigan wasn't there waiting for her. Once she was inside, and apparently safe, he left and headed for his hotel. Hopefully, if Brannigan was really looking for him, there would be a message.

"Yessir," the clerk said, when he asked, "there is a message."

But the message didn't tell him where Brannigan was. Instead, it said: STAY OUT OF MY WAY.

"Damn!" he swore, crumpling the note in his hand. He was tired of Sacramento, tired of following and watching people. He wanted something to happen, and soon.

Chapter Forty-One

Clint had to admit, he was hoping Cash Brannigan would try to kill Amy Locane. If that happened, he'd be there to stop it, and then face both of them.

He had a choice, though. He could watch Amy's house, or the warehouse the bartender had told him was also Brannigan's home. That locked door he had encountered in the rear of the warehouse could have led to Brannigan's living space. The door was solid, and Clint didn't think he'd be able to force it. But if he chose to watch the warehouse, he could have been leaving Amy unprotected.

Clint always told himself that using his gun was a last resort, but in this case, he hoped that was what it would come to. It would mean the end of all this walking and watching, and possibly put the situation at his advantage.

He decided Amy's house was the place to be. Brannigan had to come after her if he wanted the money. Clint was still convinced that seeing her come out of Culpepper's door meant she was involved. But there was still a possibility he was reading it wrong, and she was innocent. But he had to commit to one way of thinking, and that was: she was involved.

There was a stand of trees he could watch Amy's house from. It was across the street. At the sound of a shot he would have to run to the house, probably too late to save one of them. But if he got closer, Brannigan would see him.

From where he was, he would see Brannigan before he got to the house. Which hopefully wouldn't be too long.

***

It was dark when he saw a shadowy figure moving toward the house. He broke from his cover to cross the street and intercept the figure. It was somebody tall, and powerfully built.

"Hey!"

The figure turned and looked at him. In the moonlight he could see it was Cash Brannigan.

"We gonna have a good old fashioned shootout?" Brannigan asked. "Out here in the dark?"

"I guess that all depends," Clint said, "on why you're here."

"To talk to the lady," Brannigan said.

"Just talk?"

"For a start."

"So she was involved?" Clint asked. "With you and Culpepper?"

"It was her idea," Brannigan said. "She got to Culpepper, he found me."

"And how many accounts did you manage to empty?" Clint asked.

"I lost count."

"Culpepper was holding the money?"

"That's right."

"And when you killed him, was the money there, under the floorboards? Or was it gone."

"I didn't kill 'im," Brannigan said. "You probably know that. If I had, I would've shot him."

"And now you're here to shoot her?"

"Think about it, Adams," Brannigan said. "She killed Culpepper, she took the money." Brannigan pointed. "Your money is in that house."

"If you're right," Clint said, "then let's go and get it."

"She's not just gonna give it to you," Brannigan said, "You're gonna have to take it."

"From you or from her?"

"I guess we're gonna find out," Brannigan said.

They both turned and started walking toward Amy Locane's house.

Chapter Forty-Two

They knocked on the door, but there was no answer. There was light inside, but as they looked through the windows, they saw no movement.

"How long have you been watchin'?" Brannigan asked.

"Most of the evening."

Brannigan put his shoulder to the door and shoved it open with a loud crack.

"Amy!" he called, as they entered.

Clint didn't know what he expected to find. Maybe Amy, dead on the floor? But instead, there was nothing. The house was neat and clean.

They split up and searched the entire house, but Amy was not there.

"She lit out with the money," Brannigan said. "That's what I was afraid she was gonna do."

"Okay, then," Clint said. "if you were afraid she was going to run, where would she go?"

"How would I know that?"

"Come on!" Clint said. "You're already planning to get away from me and then find her."

"There are a few places I'd look," Brannigan said, "but she knows I'd look there."

"Is she likely to jump on a train?" Clint asked.

"Maybe," Brannigan said, "but not at Union Station. She's got to figure I'd look there. Or you would."

"Is there another train stop she can get to and board?" Clint asked.

"Sure," Brannigan said. "Rancho Cordova. She could board there and continue east."

"How far is it?"

"Sixteen miles."

"She wouldn't go west?"

"No," Brannigan said, "she'd want to get out of California, not go to the ocean."

"So she wouldn't want to catch a boat, say, to South America?"

"Never heard her talk about that," Brannigan said. "Did you?"

"No," Clint said, "but we didn't talk all that much."

"You, too, huh?" Brannigan asked. "Women can really get to us, can't they? Affect our thinkin'."

"Well, you're thinking straight now, right?" Clint asked.

"Right," Brannigan said, "and I say Rancho Cordova."

"You got a horse?" Clint asked.

"Of course I've got a horse."

"Then let's mount up."

***

Clint claimed his Tobiano from the livery, pleased to have an opportunity for the horse to stretch his legs.

He wasn't convinced that Brannigan would meet him as planned in front of the warehouse, but he was there, astride a black dun.

"How long have you lived in this place?" Clint asked.

"A few months," Brannigan said. "But I'm lookin' to move—or I was, once I got my share of the money. My guess is I'm gonna have to kill you to get it."

"I guess we'll see about that if and when we find Amy and the money, Brannigan."

"I never did trust her," Brannigan said, "even when she was lettin' me in her bed. But she had a way of taking my mind off my mistrust."

"I can understand that," Clint said.

"Yeah, I'm sure you can," Brannigan said. "My guess is she had me in one hand and you in the other."

"You don't paint a pretty picture, but I can see it," Clint said. "Lead the way to Rancho Cordova."

***

They covered the sixteen miles to Cordova quickly. When they reached the town, Brannigan took them directly to the train station, where they dismounted.

They went into the ticket office, and Clint asked the clerk when the next train would be leaving.

"It will be arriving from Sacramento any minute, and leaving soon after, sir."

There were several passengers waiting in the office, seated on benches against the wall. Amy Locane was not one of them. Clint and Brannigan went back outside.

"How would she get here?" Clint asked him. "On horseback or by buggy?"

"I don't know," Brannigan said, "but either way we might have beat her here."

Clint looked around. She wasn't in the ticket office and she wasn't on the platform.

"If she's here, I can't see where she could be hiding," he said.

"My guess is she's not here yet," Brannigan said.

"I agree," Clint said. "That means we better find a place to hide, so she doesn't see us when she arrives."

"We can watch for her from inside the office," Brannigan said. "As soon as she pulls up in front, we can move to the platform. Then let her get comfortable before we surprise her."

"Let's do it then," Clint said, and they went back inside the ticket office to wait.

Chapter Forty-Three

They both stood at the front window of the office, staring out at the street.

"My guess is she'll be in a buggy," Brannigan said. "Women usually travel with too many bags, and she's gonna need at least one for the money. And I'll bet she'll even have a trunk."

"So she'll need help getting her luggage onto the train," Clint said. "That should take a while."

"And what do we do once we have the money?" Brannigan asked. "Face off? Or split the money?"

"My feeling is you haven't killed anybody, Brannigan," Clint said. "I'm not looking for an even split. I just want my money back."

"I don't have a problem with that," Brannigan said. "Your account was the last one we emptied. Culpepper was still trying to figure out which account would be next."

"So he picked out the accounts," Clint said.

"Oh yeah," Brannigan said. "Once Amy realized that a bank teller lived above her shop, she hatched this scheme. But she needed him to pick out the accounts."

"And when he chose mine, did he know who I was?"

"If he did, he was stupid to make you a victim," Brannigan said. "If I'd known ahead of time, I never would've let him do it."

"Why would she decide to kill him?" Clint wondered.

"My guess is they had a fallin' out over the money," Brannigan said. "Culpepper was nervous about you showin' up in Sacramento."

"And she wasn't?"

"No," Brannigan said. "Amy is sure she can handle any man, but Culpepper wanted to quit."

"And what about you?"

"I agreed with him," Brannigan said. "I thought we had enough money, but Amy wanted more."

"So she decided not to split it three ways, and that would give her what she wanted," Clint said.

"I don't see how she figured you or me would let her get away with that," Brannigan said.

"Maybe she thought she still had me fooled," Clint offered.

"That still doesn't explain why she thought I'd just let her run away with it," Brannigan said.

"Were there any other men she was dangling on the end of her strings?" Clint asked.

"I don't know, but I wouldn't be surprised," Brannigan said. "I suppose we should be on the lookout, in case she brings help."

"There was no one else involved who was supposed to get an equal share?" Clint asked.

"Not that I knew of."

"For a while I thought Packer, the bank manager, might be involved."

"No, not him," Brannigan said. "Culpepper said he was fussy about bank rules."

"So if she's got help, it's hired help," Clint said.

"That's what I figure."

"Maybe she's bringing somebody along just to haul her bags."

"I'll help her with her bags," Brannigan said, "as long as we keep the one that has the money in it."

"I guess we'll see."

Suddenly, Clint heard the sound of a train whistle signaling the approach of the train from Sacramento.

"Here she comes," Brannigan said.

A buggy appeared at the end of the road that led to the train station. Sure enough, as Clint watched and it came closer, he could see it was Amy driving it. There was a man riding a horse on either side.

"Two men," Brannigan said.

"You know them?"

"I've seen them around," Brannigan said. "Like we figured, hired help."

As the buggy came to a stop in front of the station, the two men dismounted. Both were wearing guns and looked as if they knew how to use them.

"They any good?" Clint asked.

"They're tough boys, but I think we can handle 'em."

While they watched, the two men took some bags down from the back of the buggy, including a trunk.

"I knew it," Brannigan laughed "She ain't the type to travel light."

Once the bags were off the buggy, Amy picked one up and held it close. It was a good-sized carpetbag.

"That's it," Brannigan said. "That's the money bag."

"Looks like she's going to carry that one, herself," Clint said. "Let's let those other two boys carry the rest to the train."

"Right."

As Amy and her two hired hands started for the front door of the office, Clint and Brannigan went out onto the platform and watched through the ticket window.

Chapter Forty-Four

Clint and Brannigan watched as Amy approached the ticket taker, and her hired help carried her bags out onto the platform and to the train.

"Let's move," Brannigan said.

He and Clint entered the ticket office so that they were standing there when Amy turned around. She didn't look surprised to see them.

"Well, hello, boys," she said. "Come to see me off?"

"I came to take your head off," Brannigan said. "I can't say why Adams is here."

"Just to get my money back," Clint said. "That's all I've wanted from the start."

"Really?" she asked. "That's *all* you've wanted?"

"Yes," he said.

"Seems to me you wanted a lot more than that," she said, smiling.

"I just took what you were giving away, Amy," Clint said. "That doesn't mean it took my mind off my original goals."

"And you, Cash?" she said. "You just want your share?"

"Half," Brannigan said. "That's my share after you killed Culpepper."

"You believe him?" Amy asked Clint. "That I killed Culpepper? It was him." She pointed to Brannigan.

"If he killed him," Clint said, "it wouldn't have been with a knife. He would've shot him."

"And you think I'm cold enough to kill a man with a knife?" she asked.

"Cold as ice," Clint said.

She put her hand over the carpetbag she was carrying.

"I suppose that means you want your money," she said.

"Exactly."

She looked at Brannigan.

"And you're willing to give it to him?"

"As long as I get the rest," Brannigan said, "sure."

"You know, Cash," she said, "you and I could still—"

"Don't even try it, bitch," he said. "I'm not about to let you stick a knife in me."

The other passengers had gotten up from their bench and gone out to the platform, followed by the ticket agent. That left Clint, Brannigan and Amy alone in the room.

"Oh, all right," she said to Clint. "Here." She started to open the bag.

"Just put the bag down on the bench, Amy," Clint said. "I'm not about to let you come out of that bag with a knife or a gun."

"You're so suspicious."

She put the bag on the bench. Clint went to put his hand in and came out with a derringer.

"Suspicious, huh?" he asked.

She shrugged.

There were stacks of bills in the bag, wrapped in bank bands.

"Very neat," Clint said.

He plucked some stacks from the bag and stuck them inside his shirt. He was tempted to take more, but in the end only took what was coming to him. Then he stepped back.

"Your turn," he said to Brannigan.

Brannigan approached the bench, stuck his hands in the bag and took out half of what was left. Just as Clint had done, he put the bills inside his shirt.

Amy walked to the bag, closed it, hefted it and said, "My, my, it's so much lighter."

At that moment Amy's two hired hands came into the office and stared.

"These men are trying to rob me!" Amy cried.

Clint and Brannigan turned. Amy backed away, holding the bag of money in front of her, hoping she was out of the line of fire.

The two men went for their guns, apparently unaware of who they were facing. Both Brannigan and Clint drew and fired. The two hired hands were struck in the chest, and the impact drove them through the doors and onto the platform, where they fell. A woman screamed, and men looked around, to see if there were going to be any more shots.

Clint and Brannigan turned on Amy, who looked very disappointed.

"I don't suppose you'll let me get on that train," she said to them.

"We might," Clint said, "but I don't think they will."

She turned to look at the men who had just entered the station. One was Detective Stites from Sacramento, and with him were two uniformed policemen.

***

The local law had to be called in, but Detective Stites explained the situation to them, and the bodies were removed.

Stites had his two officers handcuff Amy and take her bag of money away from her.

"You bastard!" she swore at Clint, losing her temper for the first time.

"I told you when we met," Clint said, "I was going to get my money back."

As the two officers walked her out of the station Stites turned to Clint.

"I hope you didn't take any money out of that bag she's carrying," he said. "It's evidence."

"Nope," Clint said, "not a dollar." Clint looked over to where Brannigan was standing, trying to seem inconspicuous. "But you might want to check inside his shirt."

"I will."

"With your gun out."

Stites drew his pistol.

"And when you get back to Sacramento, go and see the bank manager, Packer. I'm sure his accountants will have something to tell you."

"Thanks for contacting me before you left town, Adams," Stites said. "Are you coming back?"

"No," Clint said. "I've had enough of Sacramento. I'll be leaving from here."

"It was good to meet you, then."

Stites walked over to Brannigan, stuck his gun in his ribs and his hand inside the man's shirt. When he came out with stacks of money, he shook his head, and Brannigan sent a murderous look Clint's way.

Chapter Forty-Five

Clint didn't expect to ever go back to Westfield, Kansas, but there he was.

During the brief shootout in Rancho Cordova the Schofield had done the job but didn't feel right in his hand. He thought about it afterward and decided to go back to Kansas.

When he showed up at Lily Claire's door, she threw her arms around him and drew him in.

***

"I didn't think you'd be coming back," she said, later, in bed.

"I didn't think so, either," he said, "but here I am."

"I'd like to think you came back for me," she went on, "but I doubt that, too."

"I came to see you first," he said.

"I suppose I should be grateful for that." She rolled over, slid her hand down his belly until she could wrap it around his cock. "And for this."

"In that case," he said, rolling toward her, "I'm grateful, too."

***

Clint and Lily had breakfast together the next day at the Harvest. Since he had his money back, he'd have no problem paying the bill when it came. He ordered the steak-and-eggs, while Lily had toast and tea.

"Do you want to tell me why you came back here?" she asked.

"I'm not sure."

"I don't believe that," she said. "You don't do anything without being sure about it."

"I used to think that, too."

"Where've you been since you left?"

"Denver, Sacramento, a little place called Rancho Cordova."

"And did you find what you were after?"

"I did."

"And it brought you back here."

"It did."

"And you're not going to tell me why?" she asked.

"Maybe I will," he said, "when I figure it out."

She bit into her toast.

"I guess I should be satisfied with that."

When they finished breakfast, he paid the bill and they stepped outside.

"I suppose you have to go off and do something, now," she said.

"Yes, I do."

She sighed heavily.

"I guess I'll go home and wait."

"I'll see you later," Clint promised.

They went in separate directions.

***

Clint found himself looking in the window of the gunsmith shop. He could see Jared Whittaker standing behind the counter. He touched the Schofield on his hip. He still wasn't used to it, but that was okay. He wasn't going to keep it.

He entered the shop.

Jared looked up from what he was doing.

"You're back," he said.

"You don't look surprised," Clint said.

"I'm not," Jared said.

"Why is that?"

"I know how men feel about their guns," Jared said. "You had yours for a long time."

"I did," Clint agreed.

"How was the Schofield?" Jared asked.

"It did the job," Clint said.

"But?"

"But I'm not comfortable with it," Clint said, "and that might cause me to get killed, some day."

"So you want yours back?"

"I do," Clint said, "if you still have it."

"I have it," Jared said. "I wasn't sure what to do, whether to sell it, or display it. But in the end, I thought you'd come back for it."

Jared bent over, reached under the counter, and came out with something wrapped carefully in cheesecloth. He put it on the counter and unwrapped it. It was Clint's gun.

"I haven't done a thing to it," he said. "It's just as you left it."

Clint reached out and touched it but didn't pick it up.

"How much?" he asked.

"Well, let's see," Jared said, "I need to make a profit, don't I?"

"Of course."

"So . . . let's see," Jared said, thinking back, "I paid . . . how about . . . twice what I paid for it."

"Sold," Clint said.

"Just like that?" Jared asked. "No bargaining?"

"No bargaining," Clint said. "Oh, and I'll throw in the Schofield."

Jared picked up the Colt and held it out to Clint. "Deal," he said.

***

Outside, on the street, Clint put his hand on the Colt. It was back where it belonged, feeling like an old friend. This was why he had returned to Westfield. He suspected as much, but really didn't know for sure until he was standing in front of the shop.

What should he tell Lily? I came for my gun, and now that I've got it, I'm leaving again. After one night. He was tempted to mount up now and ride out, but that wouldn't have been fair to her. She deserved to know why he had come back, and why he was leaving.

He never told her he had sold his gun to Jared Whittaker, and she never noticed he had a different gun in his holster. And she wouldn't notice now that the original was back where it belonged.

He would see her again, but only to say goodbye.

Coming June 27, 2021

THE GUNSMITH
471
A Price on a Gunsmith's Head

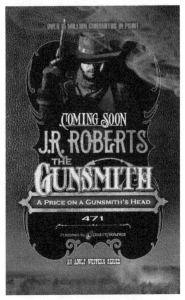

**For more information
visit:** www.SpeakingVolumes.us

On Sale Now!

THE GUNSMITH *series*
Books 430 - 469

**For more information
visit:** www.SpeakingVolumes.us

On Sale Now!

THE GUNSMITH GIANT *series*

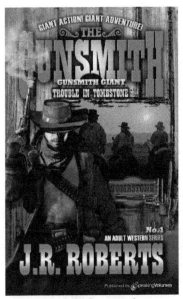

**For more information
visit:** www.SpeakingVolumes.us

On Sale Now!

TALBOT ROPER NOVELS
by
ROBERT J. RANDISI

For more information
visit: www.SpeakingVolumes.us

On Sale Now!

Lady Gunsmith *series*
Books 1 - 9
Roxy Doyle and the Lady Executioner

For more information
visit: www.SpeakingVolumes.us

On Sale Now!

Award-Winning Author
Robert J. Randisi (J.R. Roberts)

For more information
visit: www.SpeakingVolumes.us

Sign up for free and bargain books

Join the Speaking Volumes mailing list

Text

ILOVEBOOKS

to 22828 to get started.

Message and data rates may apply.

CPSIA information can be obtained
at www.ICGtesting.com
Printed in the USA
LVHW011610260521
688578LV00002B/336

9 781645 404897